Exquisite Cadavers

Also by Meena Kandasamy

Fiction

The Gypsy Goddess

When I Hit You: Or, A Portrait of the Writer as a Young Wife

Poetry

Touch

Ms Militancy

Exquisite Cadavers

Meena Kandasamy

atlantic·*fiction*

Published in hardback in Great Britain in 2019
by Atlantic Books, an imprint of Atlantic Books Ltd.

10 9 8 7 6 5 4 3 2

A CIP catalogue record for this book is available
from the British Library.

Hardback ISBN: 978 1 78649 965 3
E-book ISBN: 978 1 78649 966 0

Printed in Great Britain by CPI Group (UK) Ltd,
Croydon CR0 4YY

Atlantic Books
An imprint of Atlantic Books Ltd
Ormond House
26–27 Boswell Street
London
WC1N 3JZ

www.atlantic-books.co.uk

*Literature perhaps stands on the
edge of everything, almost beyond
everything, including itself. It's the
most interesting thing in the world,
maybe more interesting than the world,
and this is why, if it has no definition,
what is heralded and refused under
the name of literature cannot be
identified with any other discourse. It
will never be scientific, philosophical,
conversational.*

> – Jacques Derrida, *This Strange
> Institution Called Literature*

-------∞∞∞-------

*The purpose of avant-garde writing
for a writer of colour is to prove you
are human.*

> – M. NourbeSe Philip

preface

This project started as a reaction to the reception of my second novel, *When I Hit You: Or, A Portrait of the Writer as a Young Wife*. I had been frank and forthcoming in telling the world that the book drew upon my own experience within a violent, abusive marriage. I was also clear, as an artist, that the book was constructed as a novel, a work of auto-fiction.

There was not a line of falsehood in that book. Identities had been changed to protect names. Cities were swapped to expunge nightmares. I'd arranged the plot to allow for a reader to trust its intrinsic credibility instead of throwing the truth at them in the manner in which life kept hurling it at me. In working towards and writing (what I explicitly call) a novel, the artist in me was defining an experience for an audience. By describing it, offhandedly and repeatedly as a memoir, some reviewers were side-stepping the entire artistic edifice on which the work stood, and were instead solely defining me by my experience: raped Indian woman, beaten-up wife. I felt annoyed in the beginning and later angered that as a woman writer I was not even given the autonomy of deciding the genre to which the book I had spent years writing, belonged.

I therefore embarked on an experiment – an oulipo – deciding to write a novel based on a story as removed from my own as possible. A story where each influence, each linchpin behind every freewheeling plot-turn, would be referenced and documented. I was influenced by the surrealist tradition: the exquisite cadavers of the title relates to the game of consequences, where each player veers the narrative along a path of their choice.

I hoped to confine myself to the margins and allow the story to progress purely in tandem with the ideas and templates I had chosen.

The experiment was also a means of escape, a desperate attempt to use the ruse of storytelling to distract myself from an intricate political reality.

Have the margins always remained disciplined? Have they exhibited any tendency to respect my decision to cautiously separate the fictional and the real? Did I manage to evade my activism by living abroad and staying in the margins?

This book is the result of my journey of trying to find out. Come, join me, dear reader.

On a sunny day in late March, in Glasgow, we rush to the museum with our screaming toddler. Our train back to London is in less than an hour; we have decided to kill time. The all-glass lift shares our excitement, it takes us all the way up, all the way down, up, up again. Tripping. On one of the floors, we get out.

You go this way! I go that way! We catch up! I'm instructional. Museums work me up. A perky, voracious appetite. In this country they are free. Visitors free to devour ideas.

I get engrossed in a short film being played on loop. I like the mood it evokes. Dark, in a darkened room. I settle on this, decide to steal its location.

On the journey home, he looks after our son, I look up the movie.

Nothing hides mutual disdain as well as a marriage. Nothing hides a marriage-in-shambles as well as a spruced-up, orderly home. Stacked ceramic coffee mugs do not sneak up and tell others the story of unclasped hands. Clean linen sheets, in their failsafe lavender and citrus geometry, are crisply deceptive.

What can window sills betray: not the tight top-knot of a sad woman who rests her elbows on them and counts the slow passing of the hours. Who can catalogue the things that are eating her: the disquieting silence from a dear one, the impending arrival of a child, the struggle to make up the monthly rent on time, memories of dead friends, a mother whose face she cannot bring herself to remember.

Who can prise and persuade walls to reveal what they have witnessed? Holding no permanent memories, they are ill-equipped to paint out the pictures of parting shadows. Ashtrays are tight-lipped traitors. They remain smug, clumsily carrying the charred remains of late afternoons with the indifference of embedded journalists.

The whiteboard in the kitchen is hungover Hemingway: adjective-free, pruned and purposeful, displaying the timing of Spanish lessons, errands for an elderly parent, grocery shopping lists, bills to be paid – they hide botched suicide attempts, emotional breakdowns. The closets and medicine cabinets remain shut. Order creates the semblance of domestic peace. With such lingering, sultry peace, arguments appear out of place.

The space imposes conformity, demands signing up to obedience. To break the silence, it becomes imperative to break the pretence of peace.

Absence, She Said. Breda Beban, Hrvoje Horvatic, 1994, Betacam SP, colour, duration: 00:15:56. 'Concentrated on the place of a female character in urban landscapes and domestic interiors, this is a highly atmospheric meditation on stasis and movement, on isolation and belonging. . .'

Who was Breda Beban? Who was Hrvoje Horvatic? Artist collaborators: woman and lifelong lover? What else did they do, apart from this film? Knowing their life story, as culled from various pieces in the *Guardian*, I decide to fashion a character as an immigrant filmmaker in London, just like this couple.

The other character will be suitably English. That is all I know at this point.

∴

On the way home, I make my grand announcement: My new novel will be partly set in London.

Is it about us?
No.

Is it based on us?
No. Maybe.

Where in London?
Where we live, where
we lived before. Generic
London. Gentrified.

Is there something about the
time we invented the first
mojito for Walthamstow?
No.

Is it political?
No, love. It is very domestic.

·:·

Plates, hand-painted bowls, fancy wine glasses, empty beer bottles need to be knocked out of their inertia, shaken up, smashed. Fragility as a force-field does not allow itself to be perturbed. The clattering waits in the wings, romps around within four walls, impatient to join the chequerboard of greyscale cityscapes, wills itself to collapse into familiar rhythm. *London Bridge is falling down, falling down, falling down, London Bridge is falling down, my fair lady.*

the many lives of love

As soon as I have put my characters within a couple, and together in the same home, I regret my decision. Enclosed spaces call for quarrels. I feel a sudden urge to push them outdoors.

·:·

In Tamil poetics, each of the landscapes corresponds to one inner universe. Mountains are associated with the lovers' meeting, forests with waiting, and seashores with pining. That is where I plan to transport my characters. For this exterior scene, I write sentences burgeoning with a wet bleakness.

·:·

Flashback: My third visit to England, I'm home-bound in a week's time. In Leytonstone to meet a Tamil friend. He's not in. I decide to smoke to while away the waiting. I ask

The dullness of the landscape lends to their despair. The cold sea, in her hunger to dissolve everything – even, and especially, marriages – seasons their wounded, bleeding hearts with the sting of her unforgiving salt. Waves, drained of energy, expend the last of their life-force in hurtling towards the shore and spreading themselves into inconsequence on the gravelly beach.

Life grows more intricate under this heavy greyness.

It rains with a vengeance; the sky an angry spouse keeping score. The seagulls sound needy, quarrelsome, crying for pain-relief. The promenade is deserted, shops have been shut until the next tourist season, life has halted, everywhere is pared down. So austere, this artistry of monotone, this absence of performance, this impromptu penance for their problems.

--------⚬⚬⚬--------

An other world, another time bricolage of an earlier holiday – the pounding azure of the Mediterranean over the white-sand beaches at Hammamet pitted against this ashen English seaside. Parties that stretched to dawn, the coast-to-coast cross-country driving down midnight roads. *Parapa pa pa Pum pa pa Pum pa pa Pum / Parapa pa pa Pum pa pa Pum pa pa Pum.* Floating fragments of conversation from rum-drenched evenings. The sheer anticipation of finding themselves alone and together after an endless day of moving among crowds of his old friends. The velocity of all the saved-up speech, the deferred gratification of intimacy. The voices of the wind at sea, the distant lights in a bejewelled sky. Drink soaks up her speech. *You will not return to London.*

the white guy across the room if he has a lighter. He leaves his desk, leads me out to the terrace. We smoke in silence. An older colleague comes looking for him, joins us. It starts drizzling.

'I hate rain,' the old man declares. No way. Where I'm from, we do rain-gods rain-dances rain-songs. What kind of a monstrous creature could possibly hate the rain? I think. I cannot trust these rain-hating people.

'I love the rain,' I exclaim. I will not let this go unchallenged. The lighter-lending stylish smoker maintains a diplomatic silence.

I like him already.

∴

Six years later, this lighter-lender, Cedric, is the father of my children. He has now worked up the courage to tell me what he thinks about the prickly London rain. He hates it. In his defence, he says that the monsoons are enjoyable.

In these intervening years, we have both given up smoking.

·⁝·

When I wrote something based on my experience of an abusive marriage, I did not have the headspace to factor in advance how it would play out. The reception reinforced my perception that, to a Western audience, writers like me are interesting because

– we are from a place where horrible things happen, or,
– horrible things have happened to us, or,
– a combination of the above.

No one discusses process with us.

No one discusses our work in the framework of the novel as an evolving form.

No one treats us as writers, only as diarists who survived.

In my third outing as a novelist, I want to preserve me for myself. I want to create characters as removed as possible from my own life. A different country, a different love-story, a different artistic obsession. I adjust timelines,

Her judgment, her fear, her almost-prayer. *You will not return to London.* His response, neither explanation nor excuse. *You will never know me.*

Maya knows Karim, knows the love he sends her way: a drizzly-drizzly love, a confused-restrained love, a smokedust-smarting, lullaby-soothing love. Devoid of melodrama, boring as backdrops. She soaks it up in times of need, and, when it is her turn to respond to all that hair-ruffling, goodnight-kissing routine, she pays him back with an undeserving recklessness. Ready-reckoner griev-ances, Gestapo-inspired interrogations, grudges carried over from relationships long past, long dead.

These intrepid *fights* – she disagrees with the nomenclature, she calls them *arguments* – give her a lifeline into their relationship. She seeks these out like a doctor desperately seeking a pulse, two tense fingers at the side of the neck, waiting for the dhak-dhak dhak-dhak throb. She cannot think of the two of them without these outbursts.

Et plus le temps nous fait cortège
Et plus le temps nous fait tourment
Mais n'est-ce pas le pire piège
Que vivre en paix pour des amants?

The torments of passing time, the trap of peace between lovers. Jacques Brel, throaty and solid as thunderstorms, could put this love into song.

One has to breathe fire in order to breathe life into love. These jolts, this insistent thrashing is what it takes to get to its jolly, jumping heartbeat.

------∞∞∞------

temperatures, temperaments. I try to erect a wall to keep these stories separate.

If everything goes to plan, there will be no seepage, no bleeding.

·:·

Cedric is teaching the toddler to build a Duplo train. Given the colour-coordinated, complex nature of the construction, I suspect he is at play himself. The relaxed look on his face is a godsend, so I explain to him what I'm working on. He seems intrigued, he likes the experimental nature of it.

'It sounds completely mad, but it is completely you,' he says. See, he is charming. I show him parts that I have written. It is literally just the first two pages of this book.

'You have written about us.'
'I have written only very nice things.'

'But you swore several times that you would never do it.' He is saying that with a smile – and as much as I feel forgiven, I also feel like some kind of Philip Roth – selfish and exposed. In our couple, we default to exaggerations. We are artistic that way.

'Goebbels,' he says, wagging a finger.

'Bubbles,' our little son repeats, focusing intensely on his index finger, willing it to wag itself.

With their relationship on an operating table, transaction replaces trust. *Pass me the scalpel, please.* To save themselves from this oppressive atmosphere, and because suggesting sex would come across as a ridiculously selfish proposal, Karim attempts an altruistic distraction – *Could we have a child?*

It comes out clumsily.

'Do you really think the introduction of a screaming infant can diffuse the tension between us? It's unfair to the child, unfair to us. That would be catastrophic.' More emphatic is Maya's passive-aggressive citizen-of-the-world sneer: 'Maybe this is what they do where you come from, just don't pull these tricks on me!' Another barricade. He doesn't bite the bait, brushes the provocation away. Avoiding confrontations with his wife is an energy-saving measure, a kindness to the planet, ranking in the same league as rooftop solar panels and four-minute rapid-showers. The energy that he conserves, he saves up for the debut film he is planning to shoot.

He opens up about his work that weighs him down. Sharing as truce, a second attempt at distraction.

-----◦≋≋◦-----

'Goebbels, Goebbels,' Cedric says, trying to fix the pronunciation.

'Bubbles. Bubbles.'

⸱⫶⸱

Yaadum oore, yaavarum kelir, anywhere is home, everyone is kin, thank you, Kaniyan Poongundranar, for coming up with this poetry-philosophy and putting it forward to my people two thousand years ago so now a Tamil woman like me has all grounds to argue – why not this life on the outskirts of London why not this loving lovemaking familyforming with a Belgian, and, pushing this Sangam Age audacity to its natural breaking point, why not a story that is not my own, a story of other people in other lands?

Yaadum oore, yaavarum kelir, anywhere is home, everyone is kin: to make that happen learn to pack and leave, learn to filter out the superfluous, learn to dodge every fight, learn to trust your kisses, and most of all, learn to ask for help. Also, if you can pull it off: do not make rivals or enemies out of the many women you meet: they will keep the doors open to your yaadum-ooreing, the evenings clement for your yaavarum-keliring.

Yaadum oore, yaavarum kelir, one day the man you lust after will be folding your clothes and putting them in

He has to fight his professors, he has to find an idea. For now, it forces him to splice the world into frames, eavesdrop on random conversations, go location-hunting, take night buses to copy dodgy characters.

He wants to make a British film to suit the requirements of the course, not the Arabian movie they want out of him: self-disembowelment as authenticity. He needs to get the paperwork sorted to have permission to shoot where he desires – but bureaucracy is a self-replicating nightmare, he has lost his patience filling out forms. 'I can help you with all that,' she says, 'but why would I do that when you will blame me for micromanaging your life?'

There is the meta-discourse too, all the writing around the film rather than the film itself – a stilted world of similar-sounding prose, efforts at disambiguation resulting in a brain-fog. Because he does not want his ideas to be stolen, and to ensure opacity in his mission statement, he lifts word for fucking word from one experimental group or another and his instructor doesn't notice, or suspect the plagiarism. Instead, he expounds on the work and the manner in which it reveals the interior landscape of the creator: how the concept subliminally draws upon the prey-predator theme central to the African imagination, how the motif of an intemperate entity is a homage to the director's Arab ancestry.

Likewise, Karim's tongue-in-cheek dissertation proposal on the camel in cinema and the camel as a cultural trope is gleefully embraced with such an earnestness that it breaks him to summon the courage to say that he was merely being sarcastic.

He is trolling them big time, but they are not in on the joke. Sadly, satire and sarcasm, mocking and lampooning are all preserves of equals – someone like him will always be taken only at face-value.

his cupboard and just like that, without a word being exchanged, you will know that you are welcome to stay forever, that now you are a new chapter in his life.

Yaadum oore, yaavarum kelir, anywhere is home if you have lived there long enough, everyone is kin if they have held your hands through the tremendous drama and inelegance of childbirth.

Yaadum oore, yaavarum kelir, anywhere is home if you can unpack the news on television, everyone is kin when the bus driver knows you by face, waves at you when she sees you pushing the pram on the road.

Yaadum oore, yaavarum kelir, anywhere is home, everyone is kin, but if you feel that is failing you, think of all the handpicked words your mother hurled at your teenage self:

riff-raff
vagabond
loafer

and because it came from the person who made you, every choice insult became the new aspirational standard, so yes, love, you are failing at life, but living the dream. It never gets better than riff-raffing and vagabonding and loafering.

All of that also gets some writing done.

·:·

Such is the domino effect of abstract discourse: these critics carry forward his work, give it lustre and texture, lend it their white-white seal of approval so that he, animal-hearted African, desert-stranded Arabian in their eyes, can be let loose into the world, allowed to forage for the story he is after.

some trouble
with authority

I am good with creating fictional fathers; my real one defies being enshrined within English words.

This book does not belong to my father, my father does not belong to this book. Somewhere else, sometime else.

As a writer I will have to let him stand on his own, and his stories will be told in the way they must be: gloriously, with love and with revulsion, with understanding and with tears.

⁘

Her zero-hour contract job as a layout artist at a liberal newspaper doesn't have this glamorous, obsessive quality that his work thrives upon. In place of bursting into a lecture about bleed slug gutter she brings in balance to his work-is-woe talks by discussing the project of her lifetime: saving an errant father from a) alcoholism, b) bookmakers, c) whatever dangers she apprehends as coming his way.

Her mother had left them when she was too young to remember the precise nature of the entanglement-untanglement, and Maya has convinced herself over the years that her mother's leaving and her death shortly thereafter were somehow her fault.

She made up for it by being the grown-up bossy lady around the house.

She'd clean, she'd cook, she'd order her father to tie his shoelaces and take the trash out on Monday nights. She thought that such pre-emptive action could ensure her father did not have pressing reasons to bring home a new wife – a prospect she viciously plotted against, having bought into the false advertising about evil stepmothers.

Now he has announced that he is bringing home a girl, someone in her early twenties. Outmanoeuvred, hoodwinked despite keeping a constant close watch, Maya grudgingly comes to terms. She wonders why her father did not pick one of those fading English roses who turn apple into cider, gooseberries into tarts and have involved conversations about petunias. This new woman in her father's life is not one of those summer dalliances she can forget over time and lukewarm tea – she is already on her way to England to be installed as a wife.

Two decades of bottled-up hate finds an outlet. Rascal charlatan

He took perverse delight in watching me lose.

He withheld praise.

Oh yeah, mine withheld love.

A tattered coat upon a stick.

He always forgot my birthday.

He forgot his own birthdays. We would stand at the window waiting for him to come back, he would not even turn up, and we would go to bed, the cake untouched, mother weeping.

Soul clap its hands and sing, and louder sing.

Your father did this, mine did something far worse.

Fusion, transfusion, until the father beast emerges, shamed, beaten to a pulp, polka-dotted earthenware pot on his freshly tonsured head, chains around his hands, riding a donkey backwards through the streets, holding its tail. Face limp with disgrace, shoulders drooping dead. Father, father, one unrecognizable from the other. But he had a good side too. So begins another round of storytelling.

All that man is, all mere complexities.

Incapable of acting decisively to improve things on the domestic front, Karim hesitantly makes plans to mend his difficult relationship with his birth family. His father was the root cause for him running away from his homeland, and now, from beyond the grave, his tenacious grip never lets go, it reins him back, could cause his return.

Unlike in his wife's case where conflict renders itself into incessant chatter, pointless fighting, alternate myth-making and furious journalling all at once, he carries the slow-burning curse of the film-artist: hate becomes a work-in-progress, a cherished binder of draft screenplays in their numbered versions, half-formed and interchange-able dialogue, random Proustian jottings that go nowhere. This circle of family that keeps closing in on him – this worn-out, well-thumbed trope of the father quashing his dreams – this blackhole of a beaten-down childhood that he cannot escape: these are the things cinema helped him forget; having lived within them, these are buried corpses he does not want to exhume. He has internalized the idea that to make art involves masochism: the cold courage to mutilate oneself and wait for the warmth of fresh, sparkling blood.

Karim, trying hard to carry out urgent repair-work on the component parts of his marriage, finds the strength to wrestle with old demons.

The trigger for the next conflagration stealth-stalks the couple, glowing acid yellow like autumn twilight. Their anger is encrusted with the undying embers of previous fights. When the grey inertia lifts, anything everything nothing could set them ablaze. Seeing, as she does, even hostile interactions

ways of looking, ways of seeing

My father's ban on cinema and television through my childhood and teenage years ensured that I did not share the very Indian fate of having Tamil/Hindi films as a frame of reference. For a long time, I continued to hate him for that. It made me enormously unpopular at school by limiting the number of conversations in which I could meaningfully participate by a factor of one hundred million.

Worse, the insensitive remarks of my classmates: 'Everything you say sounds so filmy. As if you were repeating the dialogues of films.'

I do not volunteer the information to these petty tribalists that I've never watched a full film. I am afraid that they would exclude me even more.

'Oh, really!' I say. 'I only speak what comes to my mind.'

Karim looks at Maya through the only window he has at his disposal to read a woman of the liberated West, his own English Juliet, the visual world of cinema.

In her self-righteous, stormy moments – solid, bravura performances that have started embossing themselves upon their time together with increasing regularity – he steps back to watch the unbalanced femme fatale that she appears to be channelling. Whereupon she returns to a subdued state, and he spends hours figuring out where the other callous, cantankerous beauty has disappeared.

In her temperate avatar, she is so sure, so slow-moving with a surface tranquillity that causes him inordinate grief, vast hours of resultant boredom, and a nagging doubt that there might be an elaborate cover-up somewhere.

He has never known a more spontaneous woman; and yet, reading her with his filmy foreknowledge holds the danger of revelation: she has nothing to offer except rehearsed moves.

-----‒‒‒-----

As her lover, he knows how easily she lets things eat her up, how swiftly she imbibes what she sees in others, how she lets life's cruelties seep into her skin. He understands her special brand of insanity; why it takes her a day to get through a ten-minute short film, why she cannot account for any memory of some years of her own life.

She is someone for whom everything has lost its border, its personal private outline, and whatever she chooses to do with her life, her time, her body, these become the definitive neon edges and the rest of the world around her just keeps bleeding into a revolting sepia-yellow.

'See, that is exactly what they would say in the films. To make it look real when it is not real at all.'

'Oh, really!'

The meanness of children equips you for life.

·÷·

I am twenty-five, it is my first time abroad, someone (a Mr Tiefenthaler) is driving me from Cedar Rapids airport to Iowa City. I look at those never-ending rows and rows of corn-fields. In the fraction of a second, I'm imagining extras there, garishly dressed, dancing with pots balanced on their hips. Too eighties, too rural. Switching from Tamil to Hindi, I imagine Kajol running from one end of the frame to hug Shah Rukh Khan, in the middle of a mustard field in full bloom. *Tujhe dekha to yeh jaana sanam, pyaar hota hai deewana sanam.* I am unable to glimpse at the scenery without songs humming in my head, without transposing song-and-dance sequences on them.

Fuck my father's gate-keeping. The films had managed to find me.

I had picked it up the way some immigrants pick up a local language, arriving with no knowledge, closed to its influences, and one day, suddenly realizing a secret, native fluency.

···

A very long time ago, the Marxist-Leninists tried to recruit me. True professionals, the word recruit was not used in any conversation. They were called the People's Arts and Literature Movement. In my part of the world, political affiliations were embedded in the name: any organization that called itself People's Anything (March/Movement/Voice/Path/Struggle/Liberties/Rights) was either Maoist or ML.

A comrade came to meet me, we had coffee at the university canteen, and at the end of a freewheeling discussion about politics, he passed me a DVD. Watch this, he said, and we can discuss when we meet again. It was a DVD of *Volver*. The Almódovar movie, the Penelope Cruz-starrer.

That night I watched the movie on my laptop, weeping.

He becomes a bystander, wary, as she keeps seeing premonitions in dreams, in mirrors: dangers, approaching death. Reclining in bed, she flings cold scorpion-sting remarks about the state of their sex life and Karim cannot comprehend what she is playing at. What he sees is a grande dame unused to uttering easy apologies.

In her unforgiving eyes he foresees the acts of atonement that she unquestioningly anticipates.

Occasionally, almost as if to humour such a studious follower, she slips into domesticity, all wash-worn linen. She turns into the diva of the round, singing mouth and the waxing-waning love, and when he is broken himself, she rises up, becomes the strong woman, straining against life, eyes drained from hunger, boredom, the regular minefield of remembering and holding together. He finds this indecipherable, yet, in a place beyond words, he can sense that it is vulnerability that births her emotional thunderstorms, her fierceness.

--------∞∞∞--------

He often imagines what the world looks like through her eyes – headlights becoming streetlights becoming the flowing embers of cigarettes – life a jumpcut story of survival, love being the only consolation of continuity. He feels her unspoken, unrealized urge to be running away. He sees her in the fragments of other women's bodies: her invincibility echoes in Fanny Ardant's cheekbones, her combustible anger crouches in Manal Khader's eyes, her rigidity gets bundled into the pinned-up Kim Novak bun, her stylishness in the casual menace of Charlotte Gainsbourg's thin, long fingers holding a cigarette. Through Maya, he senses why fragmentation works on the screen; life shedding itself to shed light on art.

He is perceptive enough to see how the woman he loves embodies

No pamphlet, no programme, no political doctrinaire at the first meeting. When I met him again, he listened to me rant about the state of women and how to fight for their liberation.

What is the solution? We need to organize.

Then I went to their party office to attend a meeting, and they managed to piss me off by talking about the Tamil Tigers as capitalists who proudly displayed Coca-Cola in their press briefings. I evaded getting recruited, or rather, they escaped the disaster of having me in their ranks.

But, imagine someone trying to initiate you into Marxism with *Volver*.

In retrospect, I think that the Marxist-Leninists in my hometown were so classy.

∴

Chance is the lifeblood of cinema, said Herzog.

My chance came visiting five years ago. Jacques Audiard's casting director was looking for a Tamil-speaking heroine.

Would you like to audition for the role of a refugee?
Yes. But I'm an Indian Tamil, not a Lankan Tamil.
Oh, that doesn't matter. Someone will be there to coach your accent anyway.

Could you please learn these two pages of dialogue and show up in Chennai on this day in August? No, I cannot. I am in London now because my novel is out, and I'm too broke to fly home to simply test my luck.

Could you please take the train to Paris instead? No, I cannot. Because the visa that I use to enter Britain cannot be used to cross the border into Europe, and to get a visa to enter France I would have to go all the way home to India and make an application.

Does the casting director have an audition lined up in London? I ask again, this time out of desperation. Oh no, he's already been to London, and he found all the Tamil girls there way too English for his liking.

My hatred of borders and visa-regimes grows more personal. For people like me, things were fucked up even

this disembodiment, her Instagram is homage to rushed movement – ankle-boots up a flight of stairs, stilettos on crammed pavements, the trenchcoat that can be glimpsed in the dark glass of closing Underground doors. In her life with him, selfies to show love, to celebrate herself. The cleft of her breasts for the waiting day, the cave of her thighs for the eager night. All that attention to detail as if to ensure that, even if there were only a single remnant, it would be sufficient to reconstruct the rest of her.

Whatever he has been conditioned to believe in, he now unlearns and comes to count that the parts are more than the sum of the whole. Some days, wholeness doesn't exist. For Maya, disappearance is detonation. Vanishing is a way of reminding others of her presence. Her husband is held in thrall.

Back to the grind, bingeing on some variant of Scandinavian noir on Netflix, Karim feels that he learns more about his wife from watching her watch a screen than from any joint therapy session or remedial holiday. This is the one place, apart from the bed, perhaps, where she loses all traces of her traditional English reserve.

He thinks, rather, dare-thinks, that he has worked out how Maya watches a movie. It is a process that lacks the faintest semblance of passivity: to watch Maya watch a movie is to watch her watch herself watch the movie; it is coping with her hitting the pause button on the remote intermittently to launch into a long-winded discussion on the motives of each of the protagonists; it is the realization that she is projecting herself into one or more of the characters she sees on the screen; it is the patience required in dealing with her panic over the possible dreary outcomes she has started anticipating for every given scenario that emerges.

before Brexit. I would have felt better if I had auditioned and then been turned down.

Rejection is more portable, easier to carry around than missed opportunity. This is when I consciously start believing in the vague thing that goes by the name of luck. Either you have it, or you don't. I don't.

Later, I'll envy the posters of *Dheepan*, watch the news as it bags the Palme d'Or.

I still cannot bring myself to watch the film. It is the only Audiard film I have not watched.

⋰⋱

If I watch that movie, I will not be able to escape visualizing myself in each scene where I see the actress play the refugee woman.

How would it be, I wonder, for someone who puts herself in the shoes of a principal character in every movie? My experience informs Maya's immersive film-viewing habit.

Isn't that what all of art appreciation is: the ability to project oneself into the art object? (Theodor Lipps in 1903, coming up with the concept of empathy without having missed an opportunity to audition.)

⋰⋱

Now, for some darkness.

In my short-lived marriage, there are only three movies my husband watches repeatedly. Every other day. *The Book of Eli, Braveheart, The 300 Spartans*. First, I think that this man is totally twisted. Only three fucking movies when there are thirty being released every week.

Whenever he turns on his laptop to watch them, I seclude myself in the kitchen and escape the fate of having to sit by his side.

This must be his weakness. Who does he think he is? Who does he think I am, who does he think we will become?

I start watching these movies in snatches, with a critical eye, like a dissection in a laboratory, believing that it will allow me to learn a way to escape.

It is easy to write about it now. At that time, it was

She is the jilted lover, the cuckolded wife, the abused girlfriend, the partner left behind. She is the orphaned child, the abused teen, the bullied school-kid, the nerd girl whom no one wants to ask out on a date.

The stories she tells herself are the stories that play out on the screen. Every film transforms into a template that she can customize into her own story, a colouring book with no humiliating constraints of lines that could not be blurred.

Karim, as a professional filmmaker, does not have this osmosis, this translucence. One day, Karim can be trusted, he is Ryan fucking Gosling himself. On another, Karim is Romain Duris – good-looking heart-breaking dick lacking all remorse. When the man doth protest too much, Maya shuts him down with the declaration that she loves him nevertheless. He would have been pleasantly amused with her active imagination had he not been at the receiving end of her ongoing project of projections.

In the early days of their relationship, her forays into transposing the plot lines of the screenplay on to their everyday lives were not explicable. He had worked out that she distrusted love; this cynicism led her to dissect romance as if it were a horrific murder scene requiring a post-mortem analysis of the viscera and an Abu Ghraib-style questioning of everyone in the vicinity. He eventually realizes that she could step on to the screen to seize whatever story that was emerging and come back – hands gloved with blood and caked with filth – and make that narrative the actual story of their own lives. On other days, the same hands carry a bouquet of red roses.

In those early days, it meant instant reward. When they watched *Love and Other Drugs*, she had decided that she was the one poised to die of a chronic, terminal illness and Karim was her committed carer. She slid down, snuggled under his arm, and whispered

scary, more terror-inducing than his violence itself. Do they have scenes of beheading? Do they teach a man how to skin a woman to death? I brace myself and stay on high alert all the time. I'm creeped out by *The Book of Eli*, it gives me night shivers. *Stay on the path. It's not your concern. Stay on the path. It's not your concern.*

The dialogues seem to have been written for us. *It's amazing you two have survived out here all by yourselves.*

The films amplify his insistence that corrective violence will set me right.

The movies do not fit in with the rest of his profile, an anomaly. The ordinary Indian Maoist is a nameless faceless fighter, but the movies he worships are about a strong man leading people to their deaths. He waxes philosophically about escaping the cult of the individual, but these films betray the enormity of his ego; they give away his delusions of grandeur.

I read the films to read him.

I acted in one independent Malayalam movie. It's on Netflix, probably. It was shot in the Himalayas. I played Maya, the female protagonist. The director told me that he could not say for sure if this woman was real, or a figment of the hero's imagination. That ambiguity appealed to me. I will write about it someday.

⋰⋱

I set out to make one documentary. It never saw the light of day.

It dealt with female Tamil Tiger fighters who were raped by the military. I am writing about it elsewhere.

On May 17, 1997, Koneswari, a Tamil woman and mother of four children, is killed. A grenade made to explode inside her vagina to remove all traces of the gang rape by Sri Lankan soldiers.

On May 17, 2009, the Sri Lankan President declares an end to the civil war: carpet-bombed, cluster-bombed, white-phosphorous-bombed, one hundred and forty

into his chest a teary thank-you for being there for her. This stretch of imagination – when she had not even had flu or a fleabite in more than a year – proved to be an eye-opener. Understanding and unpacking Maya had become easier in the light of this episode.

He is aware that, being allergic to the presence of men within her charmed girls' circle and similarly suspicious of new women in Karim's life, she embraces the isolation and frivolous femininity of Sofia Coppola characters – reading beauty as truth, unbothered with patience or the passage of time. Once, as they had watched, in a state of emotional and physical paralysis, the monochrome, devastating *Stalker* set in a ravaged landscape of Soviet Russia, it dawned on Karim that in this languorous Tarkovsky film, where it became increasingly impossible to relate to the alienation of the characters, she saw herself as the rattling, rattling train.

Karim has also seen that her projections are gender-fluid – she does not always see herself as the central female character as much as she sees herself as the wronged character, the right character, the crusader character. In Wong Kar-wai's *My Blueberry Nights*, Maya did not automatically become the beanie-wearing Norah Jones who travelled all over the country in retaliation to a cheating boyfriend, she was Jeremy the Dependable, Jeremy the Patiently Waiting, Jeremy the Blueberry Pie-Maker. She admits as much when one day she shuts down an episode of *Top of the Lake* to begin a rambling soliloquy on how she might have self-identified as lesbian or bisexual (queer at the *very* least) had she been born half a decade later – and having ruined the pace of the murder mystery in this arresting manner, she went back to watching as if this declaration was a crucial plot point to decipher everything on the screen. Self-identifying with the

thousand Tamil people were taken to their deaths.

It always begins on the bodies of women.

∴

Having burnt my hands trying to make a film, I experiment with other modes of expression.

Last fall, I was teaching a course on feminist writing by women of the so-called third world. Dr Ritty Lukose, my host and co-teacher, googles up and shows our class a picture of #MeToo across the globe, and India is sparkling. It is the brightest part of the world. I could write a real-time novel about this, I make a note to myself.

July 2017 The highest court in the country refuses to allow a ten-year-old rape victim to have an abortion.

January 2018 An eight-month-old infant girl gets raped. Days later, the newspapers report that she is stable after a three-hour operation.

January 2018 An eight-year-old girl of a nomadic Muslim tribe gets raped and murdered. It is reported: 'She was forced to live for longer, so that one of the accused could rape her one more time, before finally strangling her to death. The accused then hit her with a stone, twice, to make sure she had indeed died.' Her ordeal lasted five days. Five days. A mob of Hindu lawyers prevent the police from filing a case. Hindus march demanding that the rapists are released.

March 2019 In Pollachi, a four-member gang kidnaps or entices women, rapes them, records videos, and uses these videos as a tool of blackmail to rape them again and again. The police declare that there are more than two hundred victims of this gang. Proof of a man's criminality is used by men to force women into repeated rapes.

Where does one begin, where does one end?

As a woman, if your existence is reduced to one part of your body, how do you feel whole again? I carry this disembodiment everywhere. Like a contagious virus, I pass it on.

∴

zeitgeist is definitely something he has not expected, but where Maya is concerned he knows better than to let himself be surprised.

It is her unpredictability that keeps them hinged.

To look away is easy, to look elsewhere is escapism.

And I write about here, here as in London, here as in home, because I am an immigrant: I want to make this land my own, I want to integrate and assimilate and mingle and merge and dissolve until I disappear. If this feels hardcore, it is.

Yaadum oore,
yaavarum kelir.

⁙

Another part of me rallies against this treachery, against this quick abandoning of the motherland, against this craving to be soluble in another culture.

Why don't I write India I chide myself; catalogue the horrors visited on her women (humiliated, exploited, raped, beaten, murdered) her Dalits (ostracized, lynched, jailed,

Hopes soar, then plunge like the gnawing noises of his childhood sea at sundown. It is to this familiar terrain that Karim retreats. A place where meanings exist without the words to call them by. A place that is preserved, unchanged, unchanging, in the amber of his imagination. In that denuded backdrop, his marriage resembles a creaky boat hauled to the land for paint-repair-renaming.

Everything will be fine, one day, some day, soon. A little work is all that is required. His wife's fresh little quarrels are unnecessary annoyances: he is aware of their grating presence like stray fronds noisily dragging themselves along the coast, riding the remnants of wind, unmindful of the wet decay.

Crude as it comes across, for the purposes of not having to engage with the tumultuous marital situation, Karim lets himself be submerged in his studies. Learning turns out to be disappointing; leaves him lost, bereft of even the language of heartbreak to mourn its many betrayals.

It starts innocently.

At film school, Karim is told that a project embracing and interrogating his identity is encouraged. He hears this repeatedly. As guidance. As reassurance. Peace be upon these advice peddlers. As motivation. As art statement. As part of their 'institutional commitment and mission to include a whole host of diverse voices'. Peace be upon them, indeed. What he also hears are their unsaid words. *You are here, here in London, on a scholarship, we have covered your tuition, we expect you to listen to us.* The bargain-barter system is firmly entrenched, a university is not any less transactional than the twenty hours a week he spends tortured, stripped naked, murdered en masse) her Muslims (all of the above, plus being called terrorists, plus being killed on the suspicion of having eaten beef) her Christians (some of the above, plus nuns being raped and priests being burnt to death and churches being vandalized) her Adivasis (criminalized, deprived of livelihoods, imprisoned, their lands grabbed, military presence heaped around their homes, schools built in garrison-style to house the encroaching militaries, the tombstones of their dead thrown into bodies of water, children assaulted, the men rounded up and punished for speaking out, women activists interrogated and tortured by having stones put into their vaginas) her non-Indians (Kashmiris, Manipuris upon whom she bestows the curse of Indiandom and an occupying army and detention centres and torture camps) her gays her lesbians her children her transgendered her Tamils her migrants her refugees her tourists her farmers her fisherpeople her prisoners her dissenters her writers her cultural activists her independent filmmakers her journalists her disabled her civil society her poor her dying her old her young her unemployed.

One book will not be enough, one storyline cannot hold all the strands together.

·:·

Madras/Chennai/Tamil Nadu/India
– the news I read about,
– the land I left behind,
– the old lover I tactfully avoid thinking about,
– the bitch-friend who betrayed my secrets,
– the thunderous rains my sleep longs for,
– the streets where I transport myself when I feel lost,
– the crowded, cacophonous never-ending Marina beach,
– the tiny lanes of Triplicane, poverty and squalor, ambition and hatred, where I spent the first five years of my life,
– the forest where I spent the next twenty, with its foxes and its deer, with its hares and its monkeys, with its poisonous snakes and its Brahmins,
– the IIT, where my mother fought a fierce and bitter battle for two decades,
– the Madras University,

taking orders at a Turkish restaurant.

In the eyes of the academy, not belonging to the white universal limits the worlds to which a Karim can bear credible witness. To be an Arab means to be chained to a pre-tailored word-cloud that goes little beyond desert storms and terrorists, oil and bombs, camels and bedouins, paradise and Salafists. If he could step inside their minds to play a cartographer, he would encounter the signposted landmarks for Tunisia: *Sea. Hijabi. Glory. Couscous.* And even these signposts come with conditional fine-print: only so far, no further.

The Mediterranean Sea is trouble: refugees / drownings / the rise of the far-right / what is Europe / why don't these people go to Rwanda? In another time, it was Mussolini versus the Allied troops. Now: Sousse massacre of British tourists, blanket cancellation of Thomas Cook package holidays, FCO warnings, *Daily Mail* stories of eye-witnesses. Tourism meets terrorism is a Hollywood genre – not an aspirational standard for students on scholarship. Karim's proposal to follow the footsteps of John Akomfrah in using archival footage of a World War II film (*Tunisian Victory*) alongside news clippings of ISIS attacks is immediately shot down. His other, painstakingly researched suggestion – to replicate Walid Raad's fictional archives of Lebanon for the five decades of brutal dictatorship in Tunisia – meets the same fate, as does his suggestion to travel to the poorest suburbs of his country: Douar Hicher, Kasserine, Ettadhamen from where ISIS has had its highest number of recruits. *No no no no no no no no no no no no* – the advisory committee says – *we have to discourage you in the interests of your own safety*. His well-wishers on the board advise him against pursuing this dream further – concern laced with a warning: here, we have the Prevent programme, we are required to remain vigilant about this sort of thing, the

where both my parents finished their PhDs,
– the many places where I secretly met the man who occupied my dreams,
– the city that would not tolerate such transgressions,
– the city that could give one life give one death give one misery give one the marching orders, the city that was a cruel village, a city of the meanest gossip, a city that would not let me grow, a city to which I cannot return, the city that pretended to be home as long as my parents lived there,
– the city of crows, their cawing unstilled unsilenced clamouring seizing me in every moment of my personal dread.

⁘

London is where I spent five days in labour. London is where I birthed a new life, became a mother. If this does not make a place home, what does? I wonder.

⁘

Try telling this to someone who is not a writer, someone who works overtime and works weekends: *I want to*

41

leave this city because I do not feel confident enough to write about life here. I feel irrelevant. I've rehearsed this line many times. It is the most vulgarly selfish thought to have crossed my mind.

∴

Self-flagellation becomes a default mode of feeling. I'm Marxist, my concerns and my solidarity align with the oppressed and the exploited. And yet, creating art under capitalism, I sit here, playing with form, with format, with fonts. All of my frivolous, fanciful play is the class struggle taking a make-up break.

Such indulgence, such decadence when my country of birth has been taken over by Hindu fascists baying for blood, when the country of my second life is on a suicidal mission (A for Austerity, B for Brexit . . .)

∴

Rent in London is that bitch. Every month, on the 17th, we have a long discussion about how living here is increasingly untenable. We need to leave, I tell him. We cannot carry on like this. Yes, he agrees.

institution is committed to the government's counter-terrorism policy, this is part of the student visa requirement, this would require security clearance from the Ministry of Defence, *such a morbid interest in extremism is itself a giveaway, a sign of being attracted to radicalism.* We do not need trouble at our doorsteps.

To stay political is a preoccupation of the privileged. An immigrant can be sad, hopeless, embittered, lost or angry – never articulate.

The frustration piles up. As the deadline looms closer, his options become more limited. A gesture of conciliation is put forward: *Could you do a documentary on women who wear the hijab? You could compare the women here who wear it and the women in Paris where you've spent some years.* He sees that their radical idea is merely bemused tolerance, another opportunity for the British to pride themselves on being better than the French. Karim has mixed feelings about the veil, in fact he has similar feelings about wearing socks and sandals.

As he imagines himself making this documentary, he hears his father, lazing on the terrace of a coffee shop, holding forth on what the chador meant – a screen, not a veil – and how his mysticism was intriguing and unwelcome to both the secularists and the Islamists. His father, speaking in a smoker's halting voice meant for public consumption; a voice that never broke never rose never fell.

Could he tell the story of his land through the story of the hijab? The headscarf was banned in 1981 (this, the year of his birth) from schools and government buildings – it was the secularism of dictators, the secularism that France dipped its baguettes in. The headscarf was seen as the foreign intrusion, as Islamic imposition on a Berber people, something which came uninvited into their country, something which had no right to

If we are going back to India, it has to be done before our little one starts school. It would be cruel to uproot him once he has his own routine, his set of friends, I reason.

You make India sound like destiny, Cedric says. Like an ultimatum.

I don't say anything to defend myself. Being in love means letting a remark like that slip, unnoticed.

·¦·

There are other things that demand our urgent attention, anyway.

With all of our kadhal and konjal and kenjal and kindal, with all of our romantic display of genuine internationalism, we are expecting our second child.

·¦·

First, place. Then, time. The new frontier of contention in our couple.

Not finding time: to do the work that pays the bills, keep ourselves afloat, reply to emails, cook meals at home, look for jobs, leave the washed clothes out to dry,

43

take a shower every day, call home, take pictures or write weekly diary entries about our son who is growing up too quickly.

One day he is a breastfeeding infant, the next day he is ready to go to playschool. We check out three nurseries in the neighbourhood. There is one just round the corner from our home, in a building straight out of a picture-book, green gables and all that. They show us the different rooms: the dressing-up room, the sleeping room, the construction room, the messy room. Our toddler does not want to leave a wooden tractor-toy he has found. Cedric quizzes them on all the little particulars; I just hope they will be nice to our son, not scar him for life, not break his spirit. I'm prone to such philosophical ruminations.

Back home, we discuss the many positives and negatives.

Did you know that nurseries run the Prevent programme?

What is that?

To spot radicalization, to stop them becoming terrorists. At that age, yeah? he asks,

remain. In the post-independence era, it was seen as oppressive, one of the last vestiges of patriarchy. In the worst excesses of Ben Ali's regime, police harassed the few women who dared to wear headscarves. Karim remembers reading op-eds saying the 'Arabian Barbie', a hijab-wearing doll called Fulla, was spreading sectarianism. The state set about confiscating them. After the revolution, when the people had ousted a dictator, they set about reclaiming their own space. The Islamic right exploited this, manipulating this revival and the widespread impoverishment for their own ends. Years later, his motherland, which once went into a frenzy against headscarf-wearing dolls, would provide the highest number of foreign fighters for the dreaded Daesh.

He discusses the complicated baggage of his project with Maya, and she has a singularly different perspective: *Oh, this hijab thing is another excuse for you to go and chat up girls, isn't it?*

Karim laughs at this jest-jealous remark, but he is not offended. Her jealousy does not feel sorry for itself, and he wishes he could borrow its confident, uninhibited core so that he can get heard at film school.

pointing to our toddler blissfully asleep in his pram.

Yes, at their age.

And how will they find out if this little one is going to become a terrorist?

The symptoms are displayed on a noticeboard: child isolates himself, talks a lot as if from a scripted speech, that sort of thing.

Hmm. He is already a terrorist, he says, good luck with that!

⠂⦙⠂

When I start this book, the news cycle runs around the *Windrush* generation being deported; the hostile environment policy of the Home Office; Meghan Markle marrying the Prince.

By the time I near completion of the manuscript, the headlines are about the jihadi bride who wants to have her baby in Britain at the expense of the public taxpayer. I feel seen.

Having started this family with a European in the midst of all the nail-biting over Brexit, I resist, and then yield, to the urge to reflect on the interracial nature of the imaginary fictional couple I'm writing about. In my non-novel-writing life, I'm also researching Jayaben Desai and the Grunwick strike. So much churning infiltrates my story. To provide historical contrast to the Karim–Maya relationship

Maya hears him out through the small hours of many complaining nights. She senses the stress taking its toll yet she cannot bring herself to see eye-to-eye. His grievances are legitimate, his tactic is fucking flawed.

She feels that he must seize their suggestion, subvert it. Don't complain, she tells him, it is not a British Value. Make a movie that wallows in your predicament: self-referential, meta-fictional, plundering the personal, immersed in the political, whatever you choose to call it. You don't have to play to the stereotype. They want you to interrogate your identity, use that as a weapon to interrogate them. Unapologetic, seamless navel-gazing, she adds. Dress it up in the cloak of high art.

He listens in silence. He wants to know how much she has thought this through. Or if this is one more instantaneous projection.

All that she seems to be missing is a clapboard and a call-sheet. A sort of *Discreet Charm of the Bourgeoisie*, strange and surreal, she says. Funny like *Meet the Fockers*. Or, the one you've been asking me to watch, *Get Out*. A dinner movie is a fantastic framework.

Get Out is horror, he offers.

Your life at the moment is horror, she clarifies. Exotic horror.

Maya, before the fallow, flaming terror of being with an Arab man, knew another life. Mixed-race, passing for white, zipping past border gates. Maya, epitome of Britishness who never had to face the question: *But where are you really from?* And then one day she adds an Arab into the mix: this lets loose everyone's inner Orientalist and his

in the present climate, I make Maya of mixed-race background herself. But I let a lot of the ambiguity stay. Her mother could have been a Jamaican youngster who came to work for the NHS, or she could have been a first-generation sari-clad South Asian immigrant striking for better working conditions in her factory. Maya knows her exact ethnic composition, she has possibly told Karim too, and that's all that matters.

The rest of us can be content with Google-sociology. The 'I'm feeling lucky' option takes me to this result, a blow-by-blow account of a particular episode ('Mixed Marriages', 1958) of a British television show popular in its time:

Daniel Farson introduces the problem of mixed marriages. He says there are ninety thousand coloured people in Britain. Although the 'colour bar' is said to be fading, he feels that most people would be shocked if a close relative said they were going to marry a coloured person.

Farson introduces Mr Jackson from Jamaica, his British wife, Olive, and their three-year-old son, John. Mr Jackson says he has been long-banished jinns and those nested tales, this casts a great many curses.

She knows they have nothing to say that she has not heard before. Such anticipation lends her strength. To engage is to fasten herself to agony. Their sneaking suspicion, ready-made, roundabout chatter meant to sniff out if her Karim is a potential bomber is so passé. There are questions about his family, questions as to whether he likes it here and how he is fitting in. Questions so loaded they set her off. Nobody pretends this was not intended.

Occasionally, love is a realization of porosity. Learning how much hurt she could feel when he was being slighted. Knowing who in her social circle enjoyed his company for the film-talk, and who enjoyed the idea of having a curiosity at their sunny brunch table.

Love manifests in her blank smiles when he pretends to ignore insinuations. It manifests in her nervous laughter when he makes racist jokes about his people, at his expense, in the dire hope that her friends would feel more comfortable.

---------∞∞∞---------

They make light of what is handed to them: Karim jokes of leaving his camel tied by the door, Maya mentions a harem of other wives. Karim says Maya is taking belly-dancing lessons. Maya says Karim spends his time at home making pressure-cooker bombs. They are the only ones laughing.

The problem with jokes is that not everyone is allowed to make them, and not everyone is obliged to find them funny.

---------∞∞∞---------

When they learn he is not an Arab from one of the Kingdoms of Petrolistan but from North Africa, their imagination is

feels, has a 'different set of standards, values, morals and principles', 'in many cases their grandfathers were eating each other' and a leopard doesn't change its spots. Black people cause housing and employment problems; when they move into rented accommodation their houses are 'cesspits of dirt'. He thinks if a black man makes a lot of money he is flashy and arrogant, lacking taste. He believes the children of mixed marriages are born mentally deficient with an inferiority complex. (Farson challenges this assertion.)

Farson asks if there were no social prejudice, and the couple were in love, wouldn't he want them to get married? Wentworth Day replies that most mixed marriages are caused by 'downright sex or sloppy sentimentality'. He speaks of his daughter – young, charming, with taste and discretion. He would strongly advise her against a mixed marriage, asking her would she 'want to wake up every morning and see a coffee-coloured little imp on the pillow beside her calling her mummy'. Farson says he couldn't disagree more with his views but thanks him for expressing them so frankly.

Farson introduces Michael Savage, a Nigerian with a Scottish grandmother. Mr Savage was educated at public school and served in the British army. He says he has suffered little prejudice but believes his education and background have aided his acceptance. It is sometimes difficult to distinguish between social and racial prejudice. He would certainly marry a white girl if he loved her and would not worry about any children of such a marriage suffering prejudice. He feels there is prejudice in Nigeria where Nigerian aristocratic families don't like to see their people marrying white people. He feels that prejudice is a complex mixture of political, social and educational issues.

Farson introduces Helen, whose three-year marriage to her Nigerian husband has ended. She says the main reason why the marriage failed is the Nigerian male attitude to women – they are unkind, lacking in tenderness and regard women as chattels. Being in a mixed marriage with a child they found accommodation and childcare hard to come by, which made life difficult. She has no parents but her

catapulted towards tabloid-thinking. The repressed ones speak of torture, conveniently assume he is an asylum seeker with his application pending at the Home Office, one more member of the refugee hordes Calais could not contain. They want to know if he has testified before international tribunals. They discreetly ask her if he carries the wounds of war.

They talk of white women who embraced Islam because they were being offered Nutella by the jihadists, and who later went on to fight in Syria. They gauge whether she has had a divine makeover. They are a people brought up on the premise that it is impolite to stare, and after a lifetime of learning to look away, they wrestle with their awkward attempts to inspect if she has suddenly started wearing what they euphemistically, multiculturally call 'modest clothes'. The pious horror of a secular people. On their faces, clear as a rainwashed roof, lies the conclusion that he is not oppressing her. *Oh dear, what a relief!* The Prevent programme is not something that is being run at educational institutions and large employers alone; every white person in this country seems to have taken training lessons to sniff out terrorists.

-------- ∞ --------

After the season of Jihadi John, it is the season of the chubby-cheeked Shamima Begum. The seasons of free-for-all.

Social mingling with her father's extended family and her network of friends from school exposes her to how deep-rooted the Islamophobia runs.

There is the inevitable talk of the girl from Bethnal Green. Council estates are disparaged for becoming the breeding grounds of terror. A friend helpfully sends her an email on how to spot signs of radicalization. The implication blares into the horizon: 'Do you know what you are walking into?

immediate relations were strongly opposed to the marriage. She always had to do as her husband told her, she was not allowed independence; their sex life had been good although he had hit and kicked her.

Farson points out that Nigeria has only been 'civilized' in the last few years. Helen agrees that many Nigerians still cling to tribal behaviour towards women and some of their customs (such as eating habits) she still finds difficult to accept.

Farson introduces Lord Altrincham [John Grigg] who is in favour of mixed marriages although he is not himself married. Lord Altrincham believes that the fears about coloured people are bred through the wrong social atmosphere. He thinks that those who believe that mixed marriages are a good thing should make their beliefs widely known. He states that the idea of a 'pure race' is nonsense. He recounts a recent incident where he filled in an official form and, objecting to being asked what race he was, wrote 'human – Indo-European sub-species'.

Farson summarizes. He finds it 'deeply shocking' that many people would share the views of Wentworth Day. He feels, though, that however much one would like things to change there are still strong prejudices and he can't honestly say that he is in favour of mixed marriages as things are now; he hopes they will change.

·:·

It is a disservice to one's readers if all they encounter in this book is online research. I want to find something properly Orientalist, and something that does not bleed into theory (my regular weakness), so I bring home a copy of Richard Burton's translation of *The Arabian Nights*, and begin combing through the footnotes. My findings, in order of appearance:

Exhibit One: 'Debauched women prefer negroes on account of the size of their parts. I measured one man in Somali-land who, when quiescent, numbered nearly six inches. This is a characteristic of the negro race and of African animals e.g. the horse; whereas the pure Arab, man and beast, is

Are you sure you want to sign up for all this extra work?'

Someone at her office comes up with a sly suggestion that Karim has wives and children back home whom he intends to smuggle once he has received his papers. She finds the novel *Ours are the Streets* left at her desk. Nobody forgets to mention that one of their friends, classmates, former colleagues is volunteering against *the ISIS*.

There is only so far that other people can be kept away. They wage war through WhatsApp forwards and jihadi bride memes. There is even a card slipped under their door with a crudely sketched hijabi: *Thanks for never joining ISIS.*

⸙

When politics becomes tiresome and topical, she finds her well-wishers slipping into the terrain of *genuine concern*. Eyes itching to pick fault, tongues tired with the tedium of sharing gathered half-truths, they label him hot-blooded, cite his sensitivity as a sentimental malaise, tell her he is not man enough for the steely woman she is.

Afraid to ask if he is abusive towards her, they ask if he is an alcoholic.

She cannot handle their unconcealed wonder, or the sympathy they send her way with no words leaving their stiff upper lips, as if she were a fresh wound, as if she were slow-falling to death. Those are looks that pack condolences and commiserations, and when it comes her way, her sense of self evaporates.

-------∞∞∞-------

A splintered self is being demanded of her. Unclear how to proceed, she resolves to shut out the world. She shrink-wraps her vulnerability, becomes all rustle and shine, so see-through she is opaque. Stepping

below the average of Europe; one of the best proofs by the by that the Egyptian is not an Asiatic, but a negro partially white-washed. Moreover, these imposing parts do not increase proportionally during erection; consequently, the "deed of kind" takes a much longer time and adds greatly to the woman's enjoyment. In my time no honest Hindi Moslem would take his women-folk to Zanzibar on account of the huge attractions and enormous temptations there and thereby offered to them.'

Exhibit Two: 'Good blood, driven to bay, speaks out boldly. But as a rule, the humblest and mildest Eastern when in despair turns round upon his oppressors like a wild cat. Some of the criminals whom Fath Ali Shah of Persia put to death by chopping down the fork, beginning at the scrotum, abused his mother till the knife reached their vitals and they could no longer speak.'

Exhibit Three: 'This readiness of shedding tears contrasts strongly with the external stoicism of modern civilization; but it is true to Arab character; and Easterns, like the heroes of Homer and Italians of Boccaccio, are not ashamed of what we look upon as the result of feminine hysteria – "a good cry".'

Exhibit Four: 'Easterns, who utterly ignore the "social glass" of Western civilization, drink honestly to get drunk; and when far gone are addicted to horse-play which leads to quarrels and bloodshed.'

Exhibit Five: 'We have all known women who sacrificed everything despite themselves, as it were, for the most worthless of men. The world stares and scoffs and blames and understands nothing. There is for every woman one man and one only in whose slavery she is "ready to sweep the floor". Fate is mostly opposed to her meeting him but, when she does, adieu husband and children, honour and religion, life and "soul". Moreover Nature (human) commands the union of contrasts, such as fair and foul, dark and light, tall and short; otherwise mankind would be like the canines, a race of extremes.'

∴

outside, she elects to walk with deliberate pride: she takes his hand in hers, she perfects that adoring gaze. She laughs at all his jokes, head thrown backwards, forests of hair coming to life. She holds him close, she reflects light. She shuns the looks of those who smirk at them, she reads their petty minds.

She puts on a resting-testing bitch face, she does not honour them with answers.

She does not give a damn about their widowing tuts, their well-placed sighs and twitches.

Her molten silence is shield, scaffolding, snare.

Being judged is analogous to the unspeakable discomfort of being trapped. When she tells Karim, he does not flinch. This is what transpires in a marriage, he says – the bedroom doors thrown open for leisurely public inspection. Creature of conditioning, he does not avoid the characteristic cinema reference; he digs up an old hard disk to show her the slow-zooming, single-shot *Wavelength*. Asks her to imagine this with people flooding into the room, jostling their way in each time the giddy camera jumps a little, sitting by the windows, draping themselves over the solitary yellow chair, climbing over and sitting on the edge of the bed, legs dangling, clamouring in a disjointed chorus as if they were watching a sport, their remarks pouring contempt.

Maya knows what he means.

She knows also that such sluggish response does not belong to her. To reflect with the crutch of art is stasis – she thinks – not struggle.

Her love for him manages to pull itself out from the heaps of other people's fly-tipped scorn. She fights against

What about your own story, Kandasamy, have you encountered any prejudice? The voice of Mr Farson, whom I have just watched on YouTube, hovers in my head.

Has anything happened to you in this country, Kandasamy, anything apart from being cursed at in Margate, or being mistaken for a different South Asian woman every time?

Surely you earned something from this white proximity? Farson's voice is replaced by the voice of calling-out-Twitter now.

Let me tell you a story.

I'm at Costa in Leytonstone. Waiting for my partner. Breastfeeding my baby.

A white woman comes in, sits at the table next to mine and, after staring at me for a good five minutes, asks me: 'Is that your baby?'

·:·

We will never be treated as their equals, my mother says. We are not white.

She has never left India. She was born in Addis Ababa,

when her own parents were out there, trying to forge a life in foreign lands. They sailed back when she was six months old.

Come back home, is what she wants to say. Because of the many things that have transpired in my life, she cannot bring herself to say the words: Come back home.

Is it any better there? Are you treated as an equal by the Brahmins? I want to retort, but because of the many things that have transpired in her life, I cannot bring myself to say these words, either.

·:·

it fiercely, does not allow this fear without a familiar name, this inherited feeling, to eat her away.

Something about the stone-ridden judgment that surrounds her pushes her into becoming her own memory, to revisit this cacophonous roar of a crowd closing in. The story of her family: mother languishing in this condemned state, fighting a hoarse-hostile landscape that looked at her with suspicion, hiding away as much as she could to avoid being the paraded stranger. Her mother choosing to leave behind a little daughter and a husband because it was the easier option. Her skittish father washing his personal tragedy down with interminable pints, pretending all the time that there was no problem, no problem whatsoever, and that he was fine, fine, fine. Her mother had found her peace in dying, her father, in drink, and Maya does not know what awaits her and Karim.

a good man is
hard to keep

Cedric is home, I want to say. See, home is now a person, not a place. I'm with him, I'm here, I'm home. There is no returning anywhere.

It is not the politically correct answer. Thoo! Loving a white man when we should be militantly decolonizing! Treacherous (x 12) traitress. Vetkam ketta naaye! Chee! Putting a man before your thaimann, motherland; what sort of sex-crazed monster have you become?

Would there be – or, where would be – an appropriate one-word answer? Your lover as your life, your landscape. With its origins in Old Norse: husband (the first half signified home, the second the one who lived inside; the two parts making, marking the vessel for your love). It unsettles me, this word-hunt, this word-find, its thousand triggers.

Can a husband be contained within a search box? Can these searches be customized to satisfy society?

What are Karim's categories for belonging? When had Maya started looking for the one who was going to be her man?

What was it that happened to a man, in the early days, when he had no knowledge of being deeply loved? If he never learnt of this love, would he grieve for that which was never lost because it never belonged to him? Later, when the power of knowledge corrupted him, did the fear of loss also become a fear of failure?

Did love, like worship, demand constant, unwavering devotion? Was it blasphemous to allow one person to become the centre of your universe? What if they raided religion to get some permissible answers? Will this satisfy the onlookers?

Karim and Maya; Maya and Karim. The one with boundless energy. The one who increases in knowledge, and thereby increases in sorrow. The one who ridicules the disbelievers, the one who leaves them bewildered in their transgressions. The one who is capable of everything.

Karim and Maya; Maya and Karim. The one who has made the earth a habitat for you and the sky a structure and your joints rolled inside out and your living room Ikea-furnished and your fridge stocked with merguez and your bathroom smelling of scented candles and your sink unclogged and your soap dispenser always full.

Karim and Maya; Maya and Karim. The one to whom you are forbidden to assign rivals, not even in jest. The one

To avoid the default plunge into Indian matrimonial sites, I run a search in the BFI archives: find 'husband'. There are plenty of results, but there are no answers.

The Mordant Husband. A Biting Husband. The Poppy Girl's Husband. The Husband Hunter. The Country Husband.

I Love My Husband, But!

Don't Doubt Your Husband. Hired Husband. The Compulsory Husband. The Constant Husband. Lover Kisses Husband. My Husband's Other Wife. My Husband's Wives.

Lend Me Your Husband.

Her Favourite Husband. Her Husband Lies. Her Husband's Affairs. Her Husband's Secret. Her Husband's Secretary. Her Husband's Trademark. Her Temporary Husband. Her Unwilling Husband.

Model Husband. His Wife's Husband. How He Lied to Her Husband. Husband Hunters. Husband's Holiday.

Almost a Husband. An Ideal Husband. Party Husband.

who does not shy away from making an example of a gnat. The one you call for help. The one who is aware of all things.

Karim and Maya; Maya and Karim. The ever-forgiving, the ever-forbearing. The one who pardoned you in his infinite grace. The one who fulfils wishes instantly. The one who knows what others conceal and what they reveal. The one who comes to you with clear proofs and the one who makes a covenant.

Karim and Maya; Maya and Karim. The one who does not nullify a verse or cause it to be forgotten. The one who is your only guardian and helper, the one who has power over all things.

Karim and Maya; Maya and Karim. The one who likes an offering of rum laced with gunpowder. The one who tested another with certain words. The one who brings you all together.

Karim and Maya; Maya and Karim. The one who is not heedless of what you do. The one who certainly tests you with some fear and hunger, and some loss of possessions. The one who dresses in denims. The one who shall be feared. The one who is a garment for you as you are a garment for him. The one who guards all gates and cross-roads. The one who has a thunderbolt in his hand.

Karim and Maya; Maya and Karim. The one who considers oppression more serious than murder, persecution more serious than killing. The one who enriches and emancipates, the one who withholds and shields, the one who defends and distresses.

Karim and Maya; Maya and Karim. The one who is remembered on the designated days. The one who encircles the earth. The one who spreads illumination. The one who is easily pleased.

Karim and Maya; Maya and Karim. The self-exalting. The one who keeps not from what his eyes desire, the one who does not withhold his heart from any joy. The one who ends all trouble.

Cinderella Husband. Don't Lie to Your Husband.

Doubtful Husband. Curing a Husband. Everywoman's Husband. The Fickle Husband and the Boy. For Her Husband's Sake. The Fable of the Sarcastic Husband and the Lady Shopper.

The Eternal Husband. The Flirty Husband. Her Dummy Husband. Husband and Wife. Husband of the Year. A Husband Outwitter. The Husband Protector. Husband and Lovers.

A Husband's Awakening. A Husband's Duplicity. The Husband's Experiment. A Husband's Generosity. A Husband's Love.

A Husband's Mistake. The Husband's Revenge. Husband's Ruse. A Husband's Sacrifice. A Husband's Trick.

The Husband, the Wife and the Stranger.

The Husband Who Showed Up and Did His Duty.

A Jealous Husband. A Jealous Husband's Revenge.

Her Husband's Deception.

Her Husband's Faith.
Her Husband's Friend.
Her Husband's Honour.
Her Husband's Picture.
Her Husband's Son.

Her Invisible Husband.
Her Private Husband.
Her Unwilling Husband.
I'm Your Husband. How a
Suffragette Got a Husband.

How She Got a Husband.
How to Get Rid of Your
Husband.

How to Hold Your Husband
Back.

How to Keep a Husband.

The Case of a Perfect
Husband.

How to Sell Your Husband
a Washing Machine. May
We Borrow Your Husband?
Mechanical Husband. My
Husband Is Missing. Pleasing
Her Husband. A Present
for Her Husband. Training
a Husband. Teaching a
Husband a Lesson.

A Temperamental Husband.
Worthless Husband.
Wayward Husband.

Winning a Husband.
Wanted – a Husband.

The one with the glorious neck. The one who has blazing, sun-like eyes.

Karim and Maya; Maya and Karim. The masquerade that flaunts itself. The one who can smash iron as if it were firewood.

Karim and Maya; Maya and Karim. The delayer, the expediter.

Karim and Maya; Maya and Karim. The one who is not overtaken by slumber or sleep. The one who condemns usury and praises charity.

Karim and Maya; Maya and Karim. The king of the art of dancing. The perceiver, the producer, the humble director. The one who merges your nights into the day, and the days into the night. The one who honours whom he wills and the one who humiliates whom he wills. The one who brings the living out of the dead and the dead out of the living.

Karim and Maya; Maya and Karim. The one who implores you to not confound the truth with falsehood. The one who reconciles the hearts of enemies. The master of great illusions.

Karim and Maya; Maya and Karim. The one who wears earrings. The radiant. The occasionally naked. The faultless and the fault-finder.

Where Is My Husband?

Whose Husband? Your Husband or Your Country?

When my own search is misleading, how can I help my character speak? I ransack the Old Testament, the Gita, the Quran, Wikipedia and Quora forums to find an apt description.

·⁙·

In the living room, the toddler is holding a colander in each hand and banging them together. Cedric seems to enjoy and immerse himself in this noisy invention. I'm tempted to launch into a lecture on sensible parenting, but I stop short. They are happy, that is all that matters. I don't have the time to play the role of an approval-seeking mumsnet mum. I try and tell him what I came to tell him:

They arrested. *Bang Bang*. Rona. *Bang Bang*. Wilson.

Who?

Rona. Activist. *Bang Bang*. My Delhi friend. The political prisoner guy.

Why do you have such a big smile on your face? he shouts. The child automatically lapses into silence, drops his improvised toys, closes his ears with

She has a penchant for collecting grief, the skirts of pencil shavings, Fortnum & Mason tea tins, retro cushion covers and aeroplane boarding cards from their overseas holidays. She makes her Christmas shopping list on a bank holiday in August, and has every single thing gift-wrapped by the end of October. Such obsessive ceremony over commonplace stuff is replacement ritual – she rarely gets the pluck to share her actual feelings with anyone, least of all her husband.

In Sombre English Fashion, her romantic thoughts tend to fixate on immortality – an overlooked contribution from Shakespeare to the national psyche – combining banality with melodrama, and include the likes of: *When I die, I want to be buried next to you*. Those declarations of love, like her extremely jealous thoughts, are best left unsaid.

The interrogative, however, is a territory that can be examined, even exploited. To make up for her lack of amorous announcements, she talks him into tiring, tyrannous spirals: *If an accident left me brain-dead, would you donate my organs? Would you keep in touch with the recipient families? If euthanasia became legal here, and we both were so old, would you give up your life with me, holding hands and all that? Would you marry again if I died suddenly, say, tomorrow? Do you already have someone in mind? Is this someone one of my friends, one of your friends?*

Karim, annoyed and entertained in equal measure, knows better than to engage. An answer is an admission, a self-implication; the equivalent of taking a taxi to the police station to turn oneself in for a crime that has not been committed. His aloofness gets

the palms of his hands.

Am I smiling? I'm not smiling. I'm just relieved, love. That they arrested him. Because they did not disappear him or kill him off in some dubious encounter. It is better this arrest than the false story of a shoot-out and shit.

But do you know why?

Plotting to assassinate Modi. They claim to have discovered a letter.

I do a lot of air quotes for those sentences.

What the hell?

I know. Fucking crazy.

Fucking crazy indeed.

Fucken the fucken the fucken the qway zee, our little one squeals and walks back and forth, repeating this. *Fucken the fucken the fucken the qway zee.*

⋅⋮⋅

The plot involves Dalits commemorating two hundred years of victory at Bhima Koregaon + Maoists in the metropoles (#UrbanNaxals).

A poet in Hyderabad. Two lawyers in Mumbai. Two civil liberties campaigners in New Delhi. One of the country's foremost anti-caste intellectuals in Goa and an English professor in Nagpur. The French Marxist philosopher Étienne Balibar in Paris. This bunch of people + workers in Reliance + some others coming together to plot to kill the Indian Prime Minister in a suicide attack. The plot is pot-smoking + magic-mushroom-eating + your-worst-chemical-trip + my-epidural-opioids wild. It is impossible to get five people on the left (in the same room, from the same little subsect) to agree on anything without hundred-page polemical discussions and here we are, being presented with an assassination plot spanning continents. The police must sleep more with the ultra-left, I tell myself. Diversify. Having spent my twenties as some sort of a far-left groupie, my insights are invaluable.

．∴．

Later that night, after putting the little one to sleep, he makes us two cups of tea. I complain of the heat and how it makes my morning sickness even worse.

him temporary reprieve but aggravates her attention-seeking. She compensates with apology-flowers, and in keeping with Established English Tradition: greeting cards from charity shops with lines copied out from his favourite songs. Occasionally the gauche gets to her, or rather, she gets over the gauche, and he is surprised to find entire passages from *A Lover's Discourse* painstakingly transcribed. Karim has now developed an intense personal hatred for Barthes – largely for providing philosophical justification and legitimacy to jealousy, elevating its everyday pettiness into the subject of intellectual rumination.

In the presence of other people, she remains hyper-vigilant and portrays a polite exterior, waltzes around as if they were the perfect couple. The effort required to maintain such a façade backfires, and when she can no longer hold back she goes into fights like a gladiator. When she retires from the performative hollering and roaring, her most potent weapon is the gin-and-tonic-fuelled ugly cry.

For someone with a propensity for such clockwork quarrel, she is also blessed with a torture-adjacent toolkit: an enviable memory that is deployed ruthlessly. She pesters him with her urgent need to know the outcomes of abstractions, and this confirms his worst suspicions about the British. '*Avec des si on mettrait Paris en bouteille*. That is, with enough *ifs*, you can put Paris in a bottle,' he says to her. And unhelpfully adds, 'Nothing is wrong with us, stop projecting untold fears on to us. This is like the state of your country. Only a super-anxious nation could have come up with Brexit. Self-inflicting damage.'

Steeped in his own cocoon of student life and its demand to constantly churn out work, he has lost the perceptiveness to pinpoint where his wife's obsessions about death, the frailty of the physical self and assorted musings come from. His non-awareness

Are you going to write about your friend?

No. I've thought about it, though. You see, it would be too much of a stretch. This Karim is not Indian, he's Tunisian. And their president is what? Ninety-two years old. Who goes around assassinating such old geezers? Fiction has to be real, believable. I cannot take my character and put him in the middle of such conspiracy. My agent will disapprove at line one. And I don't write thrillers anyway.

No, no, love. Are you going to write about your friend Rona's arrest for some newspaper, some magazine? That's what I meant. That could help him, you know.

I nod in vague agreement.

I'm ashamed that I've become so obsessed about this novel.

⋰∴⋱

When I told one of my Maoist friends back home that I was dating a Trotskyist, he was dismissive: 'Peaceniks.'

When I reported that back to

71

Cedric, he said, 'Trotsky was the leader of the Red Army. That's pretty peacenik, yeah!'

⋅⫛⋅

If I make my heroine an ultra-left groupie like me, this book would be full of such witty repartee. But then, only a few would get all the jokes. No one would care what happens to someone with such an obscure universe of interest. No one except the universe of my ex-boyfriends.

So, I give Maya everyday concerns. I make her relatable to the British readers. I steal a little of every Englishwoman I see to build this composite. Amy Sarah Claire Naomi Gill Lucy Allison and god yes god Kate. They are not the easiest tribe to spy upon and take notes, so, to supplement my theft, I borrow some books of pop-anthropology. To break the narrative heteronormativity of this text, and to capture a suddenly emergent Europhilia among Remainers, I let her quote Barthes.

⋅⫛⋅

I cannot make her me. Then again, I cannot relate to her finds its match in her unpreparedness. Her long-harboured intention to give marching orders, or shamelessly desert the marital unit in a phased manner, has met with the hand of fate and the seed of her husband. The latest Swedish-technology-backed, earth-friendly, non-hormonal, body-temperature-based birth control app that she has been using for a year and a half has let her down: she is pregnant.

In the fantastically linear and pre-programmed version of her life, a child does not exist, and thoughts on a contingency plan have not been mapped out thoroughly. Strangely – in a manner that fills her with surprise and self-loathing – she seems excited by the idea of becoming a mother.

So, where a more sensible woman would have deliberated whether to play host to this possible-life, and a more passionate one would have started scouring foreign-language dictionaries for a gender-neutral, non-feudal, two-syllable, shape-shifting noun-verb- adjective to bestow upon the now-embryonic creature, Maya's dilemmas are two-fold and lie elsewhere. In keeping with the fad of their times – inner re-engineering and Hygge – the first decision involves abstaining from smoking.

But a cigarette is a crutch she cannot afford to abandon. It is a unit of time: the walk to the Underground station, the length of a short phone call, the waiting for the right bus, the frozen pizza resurrecting in the oven. A cigarette is the perfect break: in the middle of a fight it allows her the headspace to stockpile fresh arguments; in the midst of boring office talk it lets her orchestrate a graceful exit. A cigarette is social lubricant, it is ancient mindfulness and postmodern meditation. To give up smoking would mean that she has decisively put her unborn child ahead of herself – and this self-effacement, this perceived loss of selfhood that motherhood thrusts upon her, leaves her rankled.

if I do not share anything with her. So, I end up making her pregnant.

In the short term, my concerns become her concerns.

Of the long term, who can say anything?

Fucken the fucken the fucken the qway zee.

⸫

Rona had written to me a few years ago, inviting me to a conference on political prisoners. Women's prisons in central India are filled to four times their capacity, children are jailed with their mothers, there is a lot of abuse going on, and this is happening because Adivasi people are fighting corporate landgrab. As a feminist, you could address this issue, he said. For me to have a point of reference, he mentioned that he had my email address from Jaison Cooper.

Jaison is my best friend of sorts, though the poor comrade would possibly blush if he heard me saying something like this. We had met when he invited me to talk about the role of the radical artist in society. This was at the Bob Marley festival in Fort Kochi. I was tone-deaf, but clearly in love with revolution more than with reggae, so I went.

Volver, Bob Marley, you get the picture. Smooth as ever, and I've learnt not to be surprised. No one tried to recruit me this time.

·:·

Jaison works for the local government, and, before that, had been an English-language journalist. With his friend Thushar, an advocate, and other like-minded comrades they were running the Janakeeya Manushyavakasa Prasthanam, a human rights organization that campaigned for the rights of migrant workers, held meetings to protest police atrocities, spoke up against the mining mafia in Kerala's forests, that sort of thing. I was a regular at their events, and they had adopted me into their social circle. When I started seeing Cedric – the Trotskyist – he was welcomed too; political fault-lines on the hard left were elided.

A few years later, Jaison and Thushar were both

Her attempts to discipline herself would not have been pursued with such zeal were it not for stage two of her agenda: to gain the moral high ground to eventually force Karim to give up smoking too in an attempt to sculpt role-model parents out of their imperfect selves. It also requires that they tide over the choppy waters of their relationship.

Alongside embarking on such a reformist curve, the unexpected discovery of her maternal condition gifts her a soothing distraction from her ongoing obsession with her father's second innings at marriage. She is revolted and contemptuous as she watches her Facebook feed fill up with pictures of his honeymoon in Mexico. The rage is layered: feminist outrage at his new bride being paraded like the trophy she is, socialist-tinted anti-globalization anger at the exploitation of women of colour, scepticism about female agency within May–December relationships.

She engages in a shadow warfare by posting links to articles on white men's fetishizing of Asian women, sex tourism, visa marriages. Her father responds to her bolshie aggression by pointing out that his new bride is an activist of sorts – precisely fighting such exploitation – whose being air-dropped into London would enable her to achieve her modest goal of making the world a better place.

Inevitably, the tense nature of her relationship with her father floats down to plant the first seeds of misplaced fears about her capacity to be a good mother. A baby on the horizon offers her temporary reprieve from her stand-off with her father – but it serves as its own antidote: it reinforces the problems of parenting and draws her into making unpleasant visits into her own childhood memories.

Simmering in this conflicted state, and as an anxious stranger to the idea of staging surprise revelations – Maya contemplates the technical aspects of

arrested under the Unlawful Activities Prevention Act (UAPA). They were labelled anti-national, seditious and, of course, Maoist/Naxal. The intelligence agencies seized a lot of Marxist literature from their homes, and argued that this was incriminatory material, evidence that they were working towards a revolutionary overthrow of the Indian state.

I ran a Change.org petition to demand their release, wrote a poem, and wept a lot.

∴

These assassination stories follow the Indian Prime Minister like a dark aura. Stage-managed entirely, they serve multiple purposes: sympathy generation, political expediency, electioneering gains, diversion tactic, witch-hunts.

The Indian CBI, styled like the FBI, found that in two of the most prominent cases (the Ishrat Jahan encounter and the Sohrabuddin Sheikh encounter) people were abducted overnight, taken elsewhere, killed in cold blood, with weapons subsequently planted on their corpses to make it appear like a sinister plot. Because the dead couldn't speak, the police held press briefings about alleged attempts on Modi's life being thwarted.

This story – involving Rona and other activists around the country – did not end like that, and that filled us with relief. At least the accused were alive and in jail.

But at this point, no one knew how this story would end.

∴

As all of this unfolds around me, I feel conflicted about keeping Maya and Karim in the safe cocoon of domesticity.

∴

how-when-where to share this news of good fortune with Karim, who, oblivious to his emergent fatherhood, remains busy chasing celluloid dreams.

exquisite cadavers

Assassination attempts on the Prime Minister's life are discussed endlessly on 24-hour pro-government big-business news channels. Anyone living within driving distance of Delhi's television studios becomes an expert. I watch an interview of the poet Varavara Rao.

'Have you met Rona Wilson?'
'Yes, I met him once at a conference.'
'So you know Rona Wilson.'

The journalist has no more use for Varavara Rao. He begins addressing his listeners having conducted his own investigation of the conspiracy. The fact that a poet had met a political-prisoners activist is used as evidence of the confirmation of the existence of an assassination plot and the TV journalist goes on to outline the plot, the seized letter, the various angles to this attack.

That things could go wrong, she knew. That she could not anticipate every outcome irrespective of how diligently she mapped out evolving scenarios, she knew too. She had made her peace with chaos.

Now, something more primordial than disappointment is chasing her down: she comes home from a late-night weekend shift to a locked home, no sleepy-eyed Karim waiting with his coffee, no love-note scribbled on the whiteboard in the kitchen, an unmade bed giving away nothing. Panic seizes her; panic, and the faded memory of her mother abandoning them without a word of farewell. Efforts at rationalization follow: maybe he stepped out for cigarettes / coffee / the morning newspaper. That is totally unlike him.

She charges her phone, calls him. There is no ringing, no answer. She calls her best friend, who agrees to come over. A text pops up, possibly sent hours ago: *Had to leave to Tunis urgently. Cannot tell you more atm, please take care, my love. Will call soonest, bisous.*

Tunis is where they had met, where they had lived their first year together, the only city she had taken herself to, on her own. It is easy to place Karim here, equally easy to imagine how he would have slipped into the role of the dejected sophisticate upon touchdown at Carthage airport. Karim with his dark blue blazer over his perennially wrinkled shirts, over his fading t-shirts, shoes whose style is ossified in time, with his wind-beaten brown-leather briefcase.

Pacing up and down their living room, trying her utmost to avoid morbid thoughts, she can almost hear him begin this conversation with a total stranger: The films you watch are

This trial-by-corporate-media smokescreen conveniently eclipses the murders of those who have been killed
– for being Muslim
– for being Dalit
– for being rationalists
– for transporting cattle
– for doing their job as journalists
– for their opposition to this right-wing government
– for their opposition to a politics of religious hatred
– for their opposition to neo-liberal economic policies that sell the country to a few rich men and drive the poor into destitution.

The mutilated corpses of these people are adding up, like bills on a spindle, and it is difficult to keep count.

⁑

Since Modi was elected to power in 2014, according to Factchecker.in, an organization that tracks hate crimes, 'there have been a hundred and sixty-eight attacks by Hindu extremists, in the name of protecting cows, against Muslims and other religious minorities. The attacks left forty-six people dead.'

⁑

I do not know when I started feeling terrified about it. But I remember clearly when it started feeling personal.

We are in Vellore, a proper mofussil town, watching a Tamil news channel on the tiny hotel room TV, staying indoors to escape the oppressive heat. I'm translating for Cedric – these are student protests now taking place in Tamil Nadu: Anitha, a young Dalit woman, committed suicide because of the new educational policy of the Indian government, she felt people like her had no future, and the students are on the streets because they share the angst and the hopelessness. I am translating the news to him, automatically, but I'm pausing in between, trying to read the news that has just started scrolling on the ticker. Gauri Lankesh shot dead. I'm on the floor, bawling my heart out, I knock myself against the walls, and I'm wailing. Cedric does not know what's got into me.

Gauri Lankesh was a left-wing journalist who published her own newspaper, *Gauri Lankesh Patrike*. She was unsparing, uncompromising in her criticism of the Modi regime.

already dead, you bought them because you were being hassled and it was your principled position to not turn away a young man hawking his wares in the hope of making enough money to buy his first and only meal of the day. Your plan was to watch them over a lazy weekend in the comfort of your La Marsa home, the film a backdrop to the cold beer and the company of vagabond friends and the chreime briskly prepared by your grandmother from that morning's catch. People like you are why cinemas started shutting down. People like you killed the film industry. Piracy killed our film industry; the regime killed our film industry. Our cinema is an exquisitely mutilated corpse today – and its murder was a meticulous, systematic process, replete with prolonged suffering, for sadism comes easily to all people.

The chiding, quarrelsome tone that he carried over from Arabic, the snaking subclause-ridden sentences he constructed in French. Alarmed as she is with embracing an eventuality that he has left her, the summery image of her husband in his element, in his homeland, is her way of giving him the benefit of the doubt: Karim smoking without a pause, speaking with a faraway look in his eyes, constantly disagreeing, most possibly interrupting everyone else's utterances in its nerve centre. Back in Tunis, he does not have to feign good manners, he is a fixture, it could even be assumed that he never left.

Before he had followed her to London, got his papers sorted, enrolled himself in film school, what existed was a mundane life of survival. The hankering for a payment that did not respect calendars. Transactions that involved multiple reminders. Begging and borrowing from better-off friends. As his filmmaking dreams languished in neglect, television became the pragmatic choice, the oxygen tank – THE GOD GIVING US THIS DAY OUR DAILY BREAD HALLOWED BE HIS NAME. He

I had never met her in my life, but I had received her love from far away. Her encouragement, her uplifting presence on social media, the kind words she had to say. Weeks before, she had reviewed my novel on Facebook, reading it alongside Arundhati Roy's second novel. She had written to me that summer, saying that she felt I was like her daughter. She spoke of her other children, the student leader Kanhaiya Kumar and the young Dalit leader Jignesh Mevani. She wanted all of us to meet. I would never see her alive.

Later, a *New York Times* story would report that the murder was committed in five seconds. Five seconds. Parashuram Waghmare, the man who pulled the trigger on Gauri Lankesh, was paid 10,000 rupees (£100) to carry out the hit.

Because she had veered into sentimentality and said I was like a daughter to her, I mourn her like I would mourn my own mother's passing. I think of her every day; I weep when no one is watching.

∴

My father had belonged to the same ultra-right Hindu organization to which the Prime Minister belongs, to which the assassin of Gandhi belonged. The Rashtriya Swayamsevak Sangh (RSS). My father, like Narendra Modi, had also been a full-timer. A pracharak as they called it, meaning a propagandist.

He had been arrested during the Emergency. He left the organization a few years after marrying my mother. I grew up in a strange setting – a fundamentalist right-wing father who was also deeply Tamil nationalist.

Obviously, these could not co-exist: my father's love for Tamil in a culture that wanted one language (Hindi), one religion (Hindu) and one nation (Hindustan).

There was another thing that could not co-exist: my father's low-caste nomadic-tribe parentage in an organization that was Brahminical, top-down. All of these contradictions came to the fore and he had quit.

He had been recruited not because he was attracted by any ideology. He was recruited because this was

worked on a teleserial, directed music videos for his broke-ass rapper friends, freelanced on a German documentary on the Arab Spring, served as a translator for a journalist making a BBC radio segment on the role of women in the democratic process. Such was the hustler's non-routine. This was how they had met.

That there are things she would learn that were not meant for her, she knew. That some of these were things that could change her life, she knew too.

Morose and grieving, the restless waiting minutes gliding into the first slow hour, then the second, she decides to look through his desk – its assortment of student assignments, three-ring binders, pen-drives and stray papers – looking for any clues that might explain his hasty departure. Harbouring a secret herself, she is rankled with guilt at the notion of invading his privacy. Her dread battles with her feeling of revulsion. Page after page after page of work, ambitions, projects, ideas – the material stumps her. In going through his papers, it is her mask that is torn apart. Contrary to the many doubts that parade through her head, the world of his work seems to revolve around one anchor, one axis.

His life's dreams distilled into folders:

FOUCAULT EN TUNISIE (BIOGRAPHIE)

LES ÉMEUTES DU PAIN (DOCUMENTAIRE)

LE CADAVRE EXQUIS (FILM EXPÉRIMENTAL)

LES NOTES DU SUICIDE DE LA LIBERTÉ, DE L'ÉGALITÉ ET DE LA FRATERNITÉ (LONG MÉTRAGE)

DÉGAGE BEN ALI (REPORTAGE SUR LES SLOGANS DU PRINTEMPS ARABE)

the only community that was offered to someone like him, from the margins, landless, dirt-poor, the first of his family to finish school, to finish college, to go to live in the big city.

They took away all my best years, he tells me now. I worked so hard for them.

They are ruining this country, he says, and it will become something beyond recognition in thirty years' time. You must write all you can against them, tell the people about their real nature, he says.

Don't be afraid.
Do you want me to be killed?
I joke.
Life is worthless if it does not hold meaning, he replies, and adds, as if to console me: At least your death will have meaning.

·÷·

It is one-dimensional to only talk about religion when talking about the right wing in India. Modi was supported by Adani and Ambani, by some of the richest Indian men in the world. To talk of his government as being pro-big business is a perversion of the truth. Big business runs this government, which is a puppet in their hands. When people in Thoothukudi, Tamil Nadu protested against a copper smelter that belonged to Vedanta, the police force gunned them down with sniper rifles. These are also the corpses harvested by this regime.

Read a Reuters report:
– In the case of the youngest to be killed, a bullet entered the back of 17-year-old J. Snowlin's head and exited through her mouth, the autopsy found.
– Twelve of the thirteen protesters killed were hit by bullets in the head or chest, and half of those were shot from behind, autopsy reports show.
– 40-year-old Jansi, who like many people in Tamil Nadu goes by just one name, was shot a few hundred metres away from her house in a narrow street close to Thoothukudi's seafront. She was shot through the ear, the report into her death showed.
– A bullet went through the forehead of 34-year-old Mani Rajan. 'The deceased would appear to have died of penetrating injury to the brain due to the firearm

There are a bunch of sheets in a plastic folder labelled 'Notes on Alienation', the contents too heavy to be cinematic dialogue, too fragmented to form a cohesive essay.

She can hazard a guess on why she has hardly ever seen him discuss any of this. It has emerged as a norm among the younger directors. Petrified that someone else will run away with their concept and sell it to French producers, they refrain from speaking about the scripts they are working on, the stories they are pitching, the footage that kept sleeping in their old hard disks. Thinking about this takes her back to the languid late afternoons with Karim's friends. Like a game of consequences, everyone parades the corpses of their never-made movies, embellishing them to the last detail. In these abandoned projects, they are recklessly imaginative: archival montage mixed with local rap videos, staged scenes of torture intercut with speeches by the telegenic dictators (their own Ben Ali, the neighbour's Qaddafi), the bread-riots overlaid on home-cooking YouTube videos that used copious amounts of harissa. A portfolio of these stillborn, miscarried bodies was an integral part of any struggling filmmaker's repertoire. Neglected ideas, fragments, vignettes, anecdotes could go around the room all day with little risk. Never having been exposed to the harsh outside world, lacking the physicality of realized films, these ghost-like creatures could travel, could ceaselessly circulate. Although these thoughts appeared pointless in the instant, they slowly added up to something over time.

----- ❧❧❧ -----

That memories can be summoned at short notice, she knew. That when they made their gaudy visits, they didn't take kindly to being dismissed or banished easily, she knew too.

bullet injury to the right side of forehead,' Mani's autopsy report said.
– The dead also included a man in his 50s, six men in their 40s, and three men in their early 20s.
– The incident was the deadliest at an environmental protest in India in a decade.

These are assassinations that cannot be spliced into the religious Hindu–Muslim divide. These are the cold-blooded murders that a state commits against its own people, cold-blooded murders to allow capitalism to carry on its glitzy business.

∴

Whenever other poets or novelists proclaim with pride that they started writing at six, or seven, or eight years of age, I'm filled with jealousy and with anger. That was not the writing I got to do in my childhood. When I was that age, I would come home from school and begin writing 'Om Sri Ram Jai Ram Jai Jai Ram' into a notebook. Again and again, this same mantra in praise of Lord Rama, until it filled a notebook. When one notebook finished, the next one would begin.

Once every few months, my parents would take us along to visit a saffron-clad, bearded, Brahmin godman in Triplicane and give him these prayer notebooks and baskets of freshly bought fruit. He would give us kalkandu and books on Swami Vivekananda. He would say that the prayers of little children are the most potent forces in the world, and that one day, the temple for Rama would be constructed in Ayodhya. Hundreds, thousands, millions of children around the country are writing these prayers, he would say. Your notebooks will form the foundation of the temple. All your prayers will help us win, he would say, and I would squirm because I hated this annoying task but I did it anyway because it meant a great deal to my parents and to this old man. And this went on for years.

Then, just like that, one day I was a young girl who could read the papers, and the papers were full of the news of Babri Masjid, a mosque being broken to the ground by groups of Hindu men of the RSS who wanted to build this temple for this Rama at this precise spot where this mosque stood. I thought of

Anticipating the worst to come to pass and tainted by worry, her mind keeps bringing up memories carrying the talk of death. How had she never sensed her husband's fatalism before? Was he merely waiting out the certain death that hung around him with all his flippant necropolitical talk? Would she end up the widow of a murdered filmmaker – the cold, forgotten story of a dead story that went in search of a story? The procession of these snapshots is rapid, random, a process on which she is unable to exercise any semblance of control.

Karim at Café L'Univers on Avenue Habib Bourguiba, holding forth on Sven Lindqvist, Europe in Africa, the cannibalization of an entire continent, the agenda of extermination of the brutes. Karim at Café Relais, sitting with his back to the entrance to avoid a nagging money-lender, passionately quoting Franz Fanon: *'For the native, life can only spring up again out of the rotting corpse of the settler.'* Karim, in the late hours of the night buying chicken shawarma or tuna chapati from a streetside vendor, talking about the assassination of Chokri Belaid, the betrayals of the UGTT, the body-counts under the Bourguiba and Ben Ali regimes, citing the horrors slowly being revealed.

Karim, telling a Danish television channel that death in Tunisia wears two faces: it is out in the open, imminent and inevitable, or it remains invisible. His voiceover juxtaposed with images of people clamouring: The dead give rise to the new, in their gruesome end they allow a society to break free. It is on the corpses of these martyrs that change comes about. When the French army besieged Bizerte and killed one thousand three hundred Tunisians in July 1961, we had no local television, no film lab. The footage was sent to Paris as usual for processing, but it was never returned, censoring and erasing our most bloody confrontation with our colonizer. Our radio, our

that temple they wanted to build, a temple standing over the notebooks filled by me, and by little children like me, and I wanted to go there and rip with my hands every notebook I had filled.

I was that young girl reading the papers full of the news of serial bomb blasts ripping across the city of Bombay in retaliation for this mosque-demolition, and I was that young girl watching the news of the RSS headquarters in Madras being bombed in retaliation and my father telling me how he knew each of the eleven persons who were killed. My country would never recover from that hate which was unleashed at that point, all of that hate which sprang from reducing an old mosque to smithereens, all of this talk of the Muslims being foreigners.

And in the way in which children cannot think far beyond themselves, I would hold myself responsible for everything going off around me – all these notebooks I filled, and how this temple-creation doomed us all, and because I was still a child, I hated myself, my religion, I stopped praying to gods unless I was really scared at night, and I resolved that I would marry a Muslim, marry a Christian just so that my love would undo the hate that was all around us.

⁂

Some days, the writing that I am doing now seems like the equivalent of pressing Ctrl+Z a thousand times. Undo, undo, undo.

I take refuge in fiction, in forging a Maya and a Karim, in telling their story to you, in keeping you entertained.

⁂

Even if all the hate around us comes undone, what will become of those who were killed? They will never be brought back to life. And if we do nothing to challenge this atmosphere of hate, they will have died in vain. Their inert corpses will mock and mock our inaction.

⁂

cinema, our television – it was all born on the dismembered, unremembered bodies of these Tunisians. We will never forget this. It was on the body, the self-immolated body of Mohamed Bouazizi, that the Arab Spring happened. The dead we bury are the seeds of our revolutions.

Over café direct, and in the company of his friends, this talk had appeared political, visionary, emotional. Now, remembering it makes Maya come too close to horror, almost pushes her over the edge.

⸺⸺⸺◦◦◦⸺⸺⸺

In her listlessness, she desperately wishes to establish contact with his estranged family. She scrolls through the contacts on her phone. She is ashamed to realize how little she has engaged with them, how scanty her knowledge of them remains. Only their first names, what they do for a living, their particular weaknesses as observed by Karim. The lack of a common language and a troubled history from her husband has held them all apart: the two sides of a frightening laceration, unable to come together, unable to heal.

At that precise moment, her phone lights up and his call comes through.

strangers in the night

'Listen, my love, Youssef's alive, that's the only good news I can give you.

He's been arrested, we don't yet know where they are holding him. You know how it is – I am in the dark – some say it could be the prison at Kairoun but just now Aziz texted me saying it could be a secret detention centre on the outskirts of the city – I am doing all I can – it is not easy, it looks like they have been after his ass for a while.

I do not even know the whole picture – merde – it is so fucked up and crazy, Maya – this whole country is a prison – it is tragic, maama's first words to me were let us go to the police and find out what happened to him and yallah – my reaction was putain zebbi zebbi – having to swear at her – what could I say to her: the police are the ones hunting her little son down, the police raped his friend, the police are now beating him to an inch of his life somewhere and may even kill him to cover up their crimes – I've told her he is possibly on a surprise holiday with his friends.

I'm buying time, not sending her into a panic, doing what can be done.

I am sorry I had to rush here – I couldn't reach you – couldn't think through –

And you better set up that voice-mail on your phone, one never knows what happens in an emergency until we are actually in the middle of one – I was paralysed really – I am –

All this feels like a nightmare without end –

We do not even know the charges they are pressing: we are lucky if it is hash possession and that is already a year in prison – but they may go all the way, frame him as a terrorist, do what it takes to ensure his silence.'

She listens to his voice break,
  she listens to him cry
  she closes her eyes
  and imagines the two brothers
feeding stray cats on their terrace
chasing one another through the
endless alleyways around their home
playing games playing rap battles
playing adults until the light fell the
honey-warmth of a shared childhood

  she can decipher in his franco-
arabic swearing the pent-up anger
against his father – a fence-sitter who
worked in shady jobs –

  the shame of a loser son who could
not make it in Tunis
  who could not make it in Paris
  she can feel his hot tears
  the redeeming fight
  against constantly being seen as the
elder son who did not marry a girl from
his mother's island of Djerba
  against being seen as the comrade

who did not stay behind to fight the good fight

and his speech is muffled

and she does not follow a word of what he says but she knows that lost somewhere

in all these challenges, all his agenda of vanquishing the injustices of this world,

there lies the faltering tone of a man who wants his love by his side.

And the ceaseless thoughts run through Maya's head: What's the worst that could happen if I went? What's the worst that could happen if I stayed behind?

What's the worst that could happen to them?

That Youssef would be tortured, imprisoned for years, imprisoned without trial, murdered even, and this would break Karim, it would push him neck deep into fighting for his release, but it would be better for her to go there, to remain with him, to give him moral support, to give him strength, to help him strategize.

What's the worst that could happen?

That Karim could be arrested for asking too many questions, that he could be arrested for being brash to the police when he goes looking for his brother demanding his release, that Karim could be held under the drug law, under the sodomy law, under the terrorism law, but it would be better for her to stay in the loop, to be his family's first point of contact, to be the foreigner they can rely on, the person who might know journalists in other lands, the person who could help bring this story to the eyes of the world, the teary wife demanding justice in a short minute-long video that goes viral on social media.

What's the worst that could happen?

That Karim would never return to London, that the events of the recent period would propel him into organizing on the ground in Tunis, that their little work-in-progress family could be torn asunder even before it came into being, and, in that case, it would make sense for her to join him, it would be the right thing for the child who would be better off knowing their father in the flesh and blood.

What's the worst worst thing that could happen?

That things could get bleak before they got better, that things could radically degenerate from one day to the next, that the culture of extra-judicial killings would rear its head again, that Karim would have to pay with his life for the freedom that he believed in, and Maya does not know how to grapple with that – just the thought of letting him choose a path that might lead to his death frightens her – and she does not know what to do but to blame him and silent-scream (what can I do, what do I do then?), and feeling stronger that at least if she went there, she could dissuade him, she could teach him some tact, some diplomacy, that her presence would miraculously make him more cautious in his movements, and she could pray with all her life that he will come home every evening unhurt, unkilled, and she would have his loud, contented breathing in her bed at night, she would have his face to wake up to in the mornings and in the end her choices would not be in vain.

What's the worst that could happen?
What's the worst that could happen?
What's the worst that could happen?
What's the worst that could happen?
What's the worst that could happen?
What's the worst that could happen?

It is a question that eats her head in neat little circles. It is a question to which she wants to exhaust all the answers.

It is a question she will visit again and again until she has killed it.

It is a question that she asks herself because she wants to know how far she will go for love.

It is a question that she asks herself because she wants to know how much she will give up for the struggle.

It is a question that will self-destruct when there is nothing but silence from Karim's side.

What's the worst that could happen?
What's the worst that could happen?
What's the worst that could happen?

It is a question that multiplies its own presence.

What's the worst that could happen?
What's the worst that could happen?

Anything.
Anything really.
Brace yourself.

It is a question that is a dare.

It is a question that will not let her be unless she speaks the words it needs to hear:

let me go,

let us see

what comes afterwards.

---

acknowledgements

This book would not have been possible to imagine, inhabit or write if I did not have Cedric in my life. Every book is for you, and for our little ones.

This book is dedicated to you, Poppy Mostyn-Owen, my editor. You showed me what was possible, and you did not suffer self-indulgence. For that, I'm indebted to you.

Thanks to my amma for the lessons in patience, for seeing me through my sad days, and for teaching me the fine art of stealing time. Miriam, now my maman too, for looking after me, for being the voice of sanity in my life. Thank you, appa. One day, I will make you proud of me. Thank you, dearest sister Thenral, for all the usual, unsaid reasons.

Thank you, Laura Fitzgerald and Nimmi Gowrinathan: no one could ask for stronger friends.

To Jaison 'Cooper maaman'. To all the comrades I've known in India and everywhere else, for sharpening my understanding of struggle, for replenishing my faith in the fight against capitalism.

Among the writer-artist friends in India, thanks to Malathi Maithri, S. Anand, Manash Arya, Sam Arni. Most urgently, my thanks to Advocate R. Natarajan who fights on my behalf like my own father would. In Tunis, my special thanks to my friend Amina. To the other comrades there who are fighting for a better future: Aymen, Ftouh, Yassine.

For all the amazing women who made great efforts to get me the time to write or the money to pay the rent: Ritty Lukose at NYU Gallatin. Sarah Hodges at Warwick. Sandeep Parmar at Liverpool. Deborah Smith at Tilted Axis Press. I look up to you and send you my awkward thanks in the form of this book.

I could not have continued my life as a writer without the enduring support of David Godwin and Heather Godwin. Thank you, Lisette Verhagen and Philippa Sitters at DGA – for the kind words you always have for me. For the supreme act of faith: special thanks to James Roxburgh – editor-publisher with the bungee-jumper's sense of risk-taking. And my gratitude to you, Kirsty Doole: in another life I want to live across the street from you – and share this love of books, this life of being a mother.

Thank you, Richard Carr, for your brilliant attention to detail – your layout has brought this book to life. Thank you, Carmen R. Balit, for such a badass cover.

Above all else, this history of struggle belongs to the many activists and writers and advocates who are now in India's prisons – falsely jailed for trying to create a more equal country. In particular, Dr Anand Teltumbde and the imprisoned Bhima Koregaon 9: Rona Wilson, Varavara Rao, Sudha Bharadwaj, Vernon Gonsalves, Shoma Sen, Surendra Gadling, Sudhir Dhawale, Arun Ferreira and Mahesh Raut.

All words are hideously poor shadows for the price that is being paid with lives.

April 10, 2019